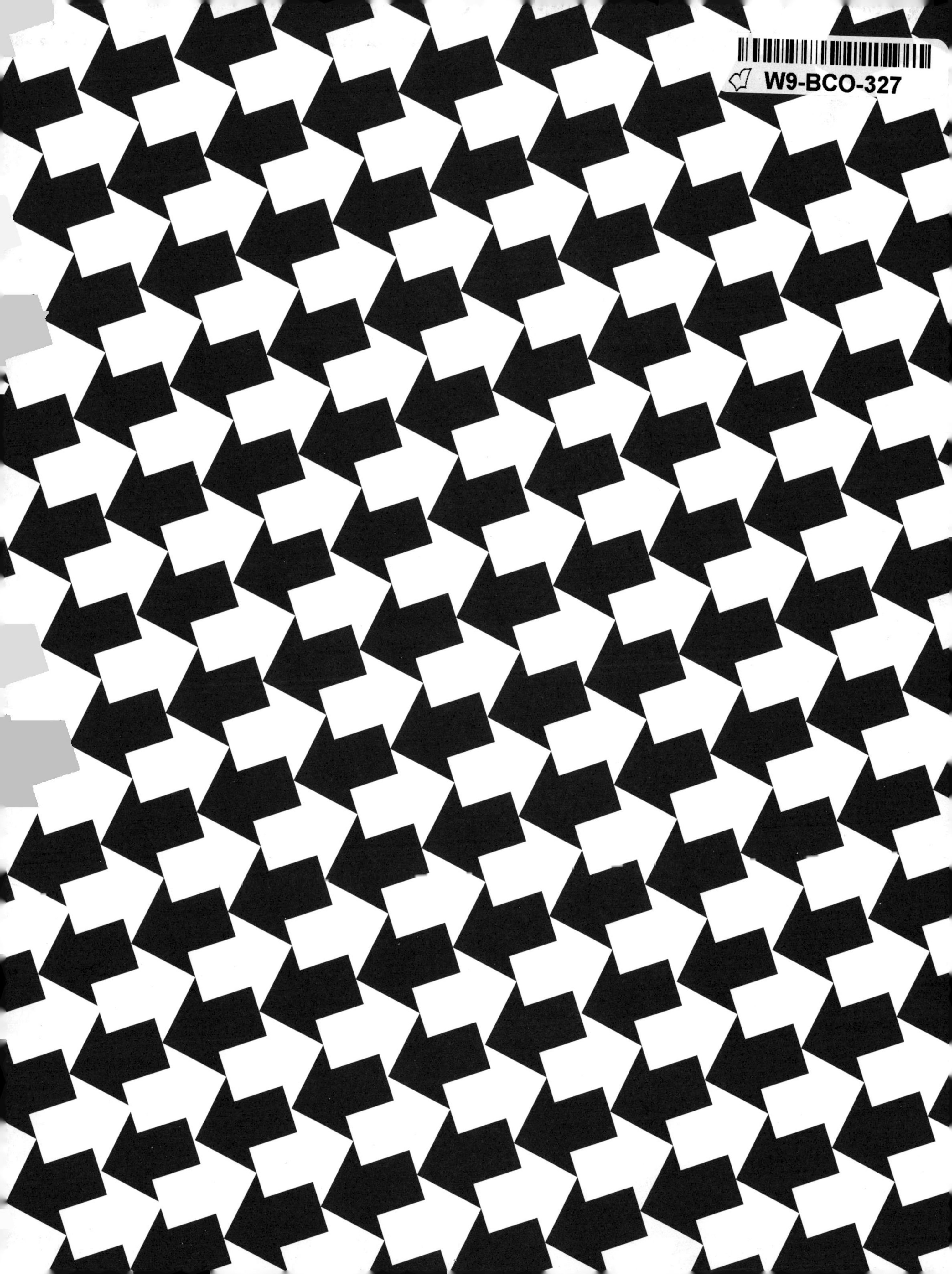

OPTICAL ILLUSIONS

OPTICAL ILLUSIONS

OVER **150** DECEPTIVE IMAGES TO BEND YOUR MIND

Dr Gareth Moore

Bath • New York • Singapore • Hong Kong • Cologne • Delhi
Melbourne • Amsterdam • Johannesburg • Shenzhen

This edition published by Parragon Books Ltd 2013 and distributed by

Parragon Inc.
440 Park Avenue South, 13th Floor
New York, NY 10016
www.parragon.com

Written by and all illusions by Dr Gareth Moore

ISBN 978-1-4723-3095-6

Printed in China

Put On Your Safety Goggles

Get ready to experience the limits of your visual system.

Prepare to wend your way through a giddying array of optical illusions. Welcome to the place where objects vanish, straight lines bend, colors change, stationary items move, and identical shapes look different.

You might already have spotted the handy "visual interpreter" tucked into the front of the book. It will help you decide whether an illusion is real or not. But here's a hint—they're all real! Look out for these decoder symbols, which identify the best interpreter tool to use:

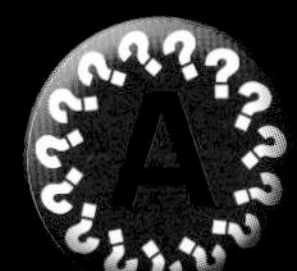

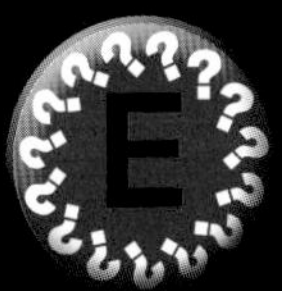

And the safety goggles? If an illusion starts to make you feel ill or in any way unwell then don't just keep staring—put the book down, close your eyes for a minute and try again later. It's good advice.

Let the confusion begin by turning to the illusion type of your choice:

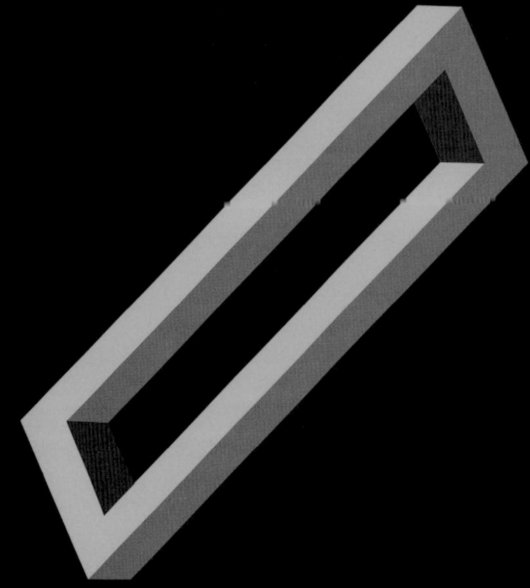

Curving In and Out

Do these lines bend?

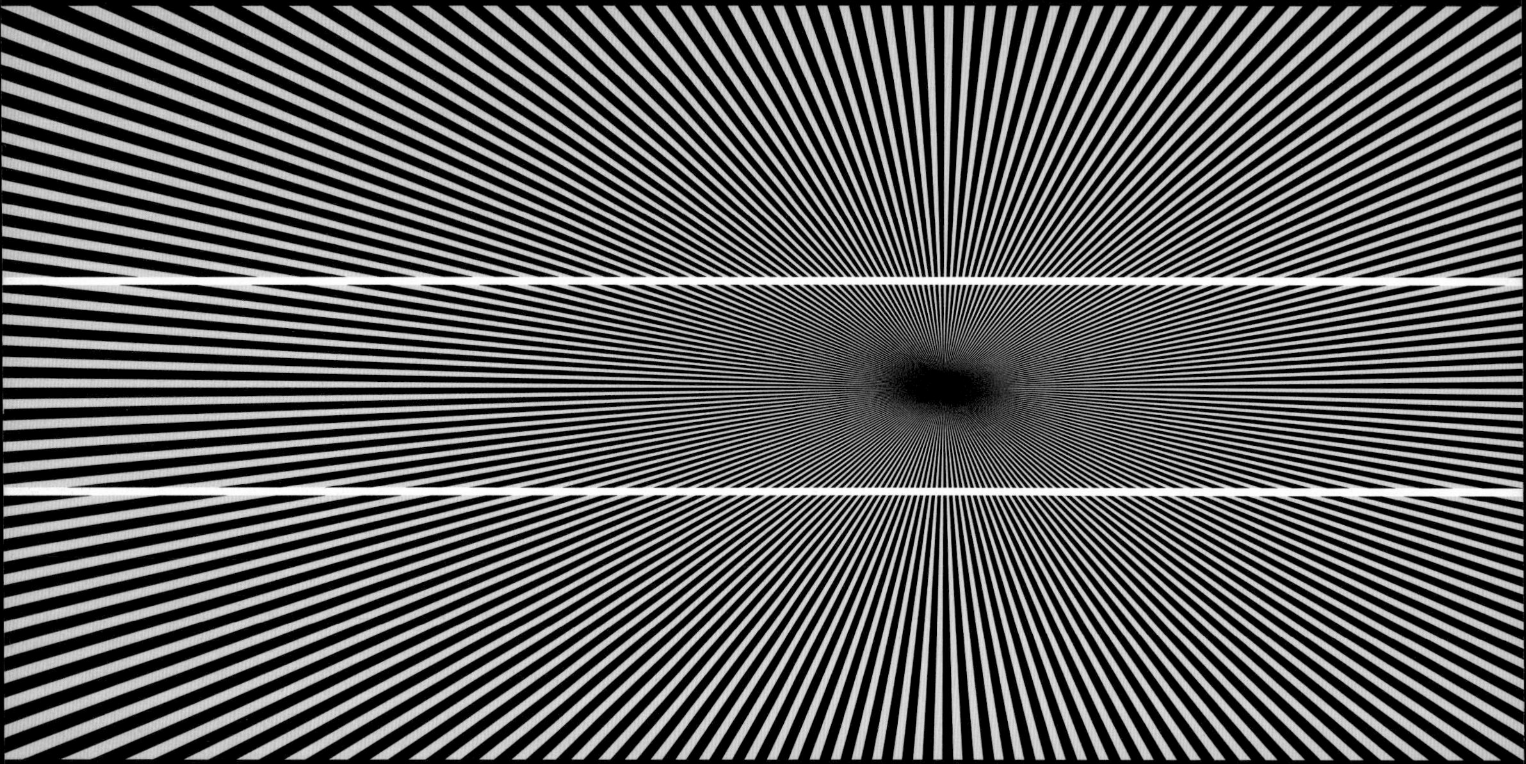

Although the white lines above appear to curve outwards and then back in as they run from left to right, it's just an optical illusion. In other words, your brain is tricking you.

Place decoder A over the lines to prove that both are perfectly straight.

In the illustration to the left, the blue lines appear to suck in towards the center of the circle, but again this is an illusion. Each of the blue-lined shapes is a perfect square.

Your brain is treating the nested circles as a tunnel, incorrectly assuming that the squares bend in with distance.

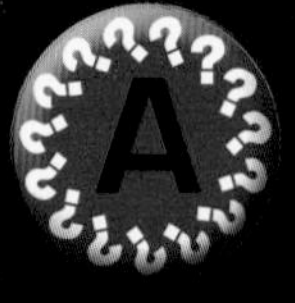

Standing Straight

Are these standing and fallen fences parallel with one another?

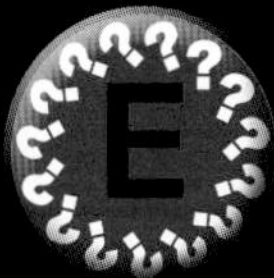

If you thought the illusions opposite were surprising, you might find this staggering. It seems obvious that the diagonal lines above converge and diverge as they travel across the picture, and yet if you measure the separations at the top and bottom with decoder E you'll discover they do no such thing. They're all perfect parallel lines.

And just as the squares on the opposite page seem to suck in towards the center, so the rotated square to the right appears to curve outwards.

No matter how hard you try you won't be able to stop your brain processing images such as these in this way—it's part of the initial image processing that happens before the details get anywhere near your conscious mind.

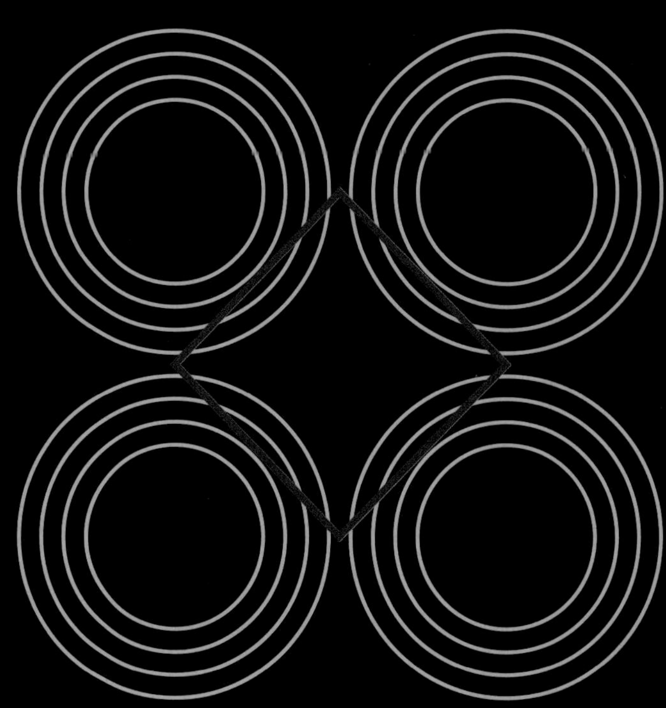

Bending the Truth

Are these perfectly square checkerboard patterns?

Many of the lines in this upper grid seem to tilt and bend as they pass by the circular segments. This happens as your brain tries desperately to line up elements which don't actually line up at all.

A

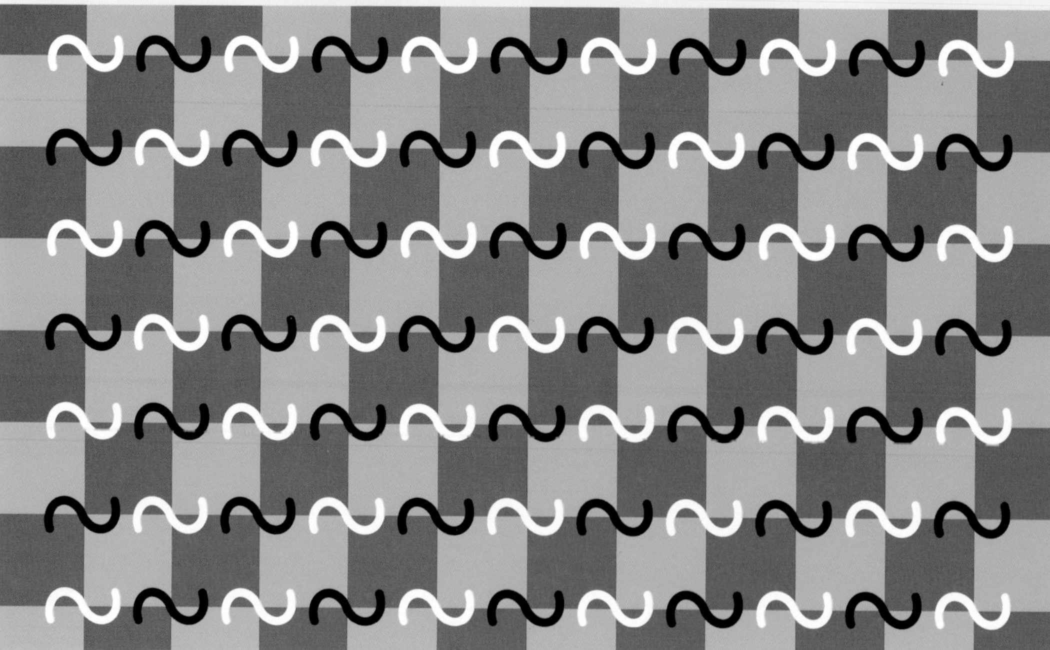

In this blue and green grid the curves lend the suggestion of a gentle downward tilt to the horizontal rows. Despite the visual strength of the regular checkerboard layout, the central sweep of each curve makes your visual system infer that the underlying checkerboard is angled. Measure with decoder E to ensure there is no such tilt.

E

A Simple *Diversion*

Are these black lines between the checkered diagonals straight or do they bend?

The main black diagonals appear to undulate as they run across and up the page, but if you use one of the straight line slits in decoder A to test, you will discover that they are all perfect straight lines. The offset checkerboard pattern is so visually dominant it makes the less prominent element appear distorted.

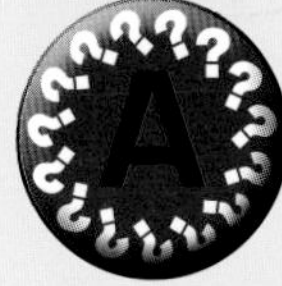

Diagonals

Adding markers to checkerboard pieces, above, or shading the interiors, below, adds weight to the squares and causes the eye to perceive a distortion of the straight edges even when there is in fact none.

Use decoder A to see that all of the lines are perfectly straight.

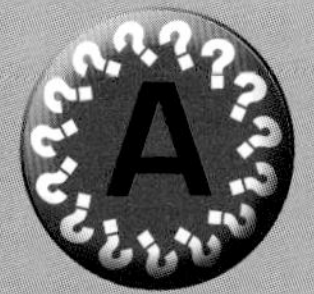

Background Distortion

Can you ignore the backgrounds and decide if the lines are straight?

The lines in the above picture seem to bend and diverge, but in reality they are all parallel to one another. The brain is overcompensating for the angled lines in the background, causing distortions in the foreground lines. The same happens in the picture below, but you may also see ghostly colors along the contours. Try rotating the book a quarter turn and the colors will jump to their neighboring lines.

A Sense of **Proportion**

Are these central shapes and arrows different sizes?

The two yellow circles appear to be different sizes, as do the two green squares below. But are they really? Use decoder B to check both.

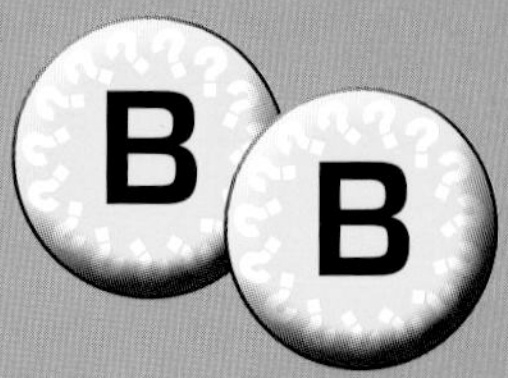

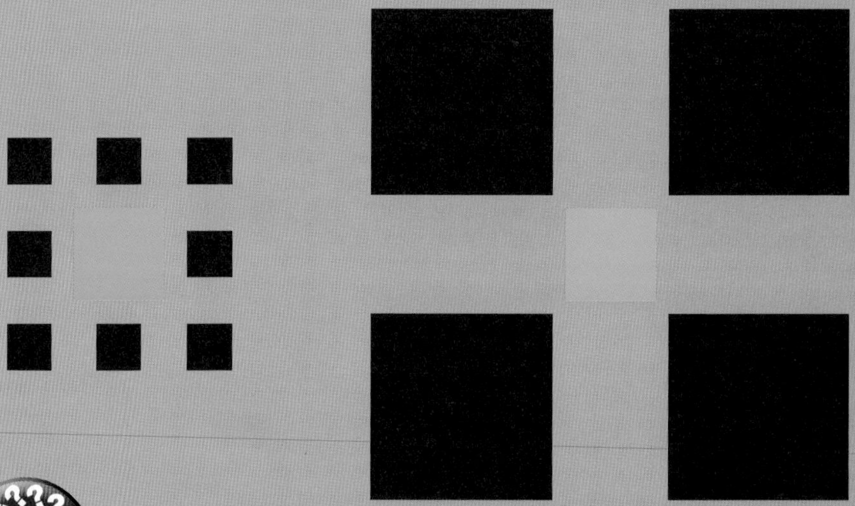

One of the most famous optical illusions is illustrated by the black arrows below. The upper arrow appears to be shorter than the lower arrow, although in fact they are the same length.

This illusion can be strengthened further still by adding additional depth cues, as in the yellow wall illusion to the right. Remarkably, both red arrows are exactly the same length.

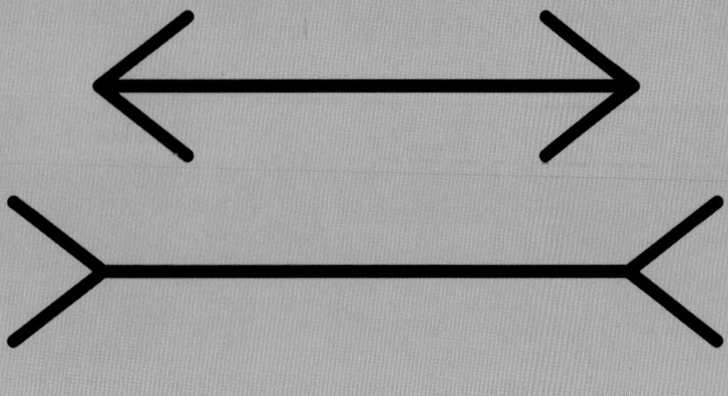

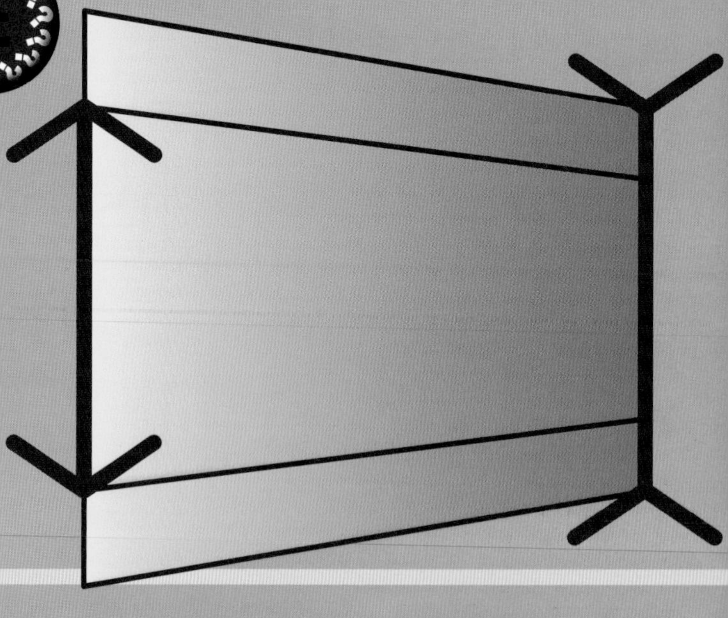

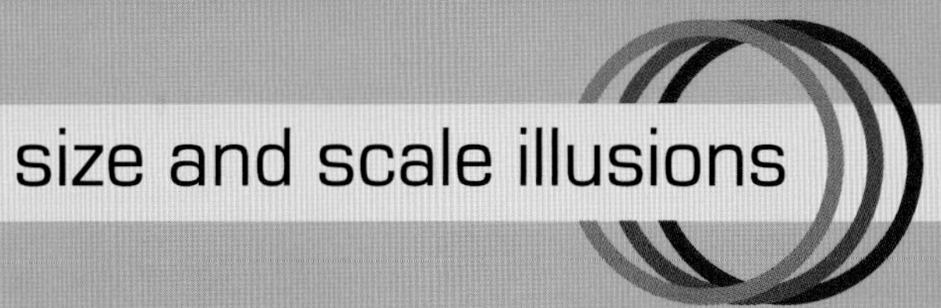

Rectangular *Confusion*

Which of these horizontal rectangles precisely matches the uppermost, vertical rectangle?

One of the human brain's more inaccurate optical analysis procedures takes place when you look at something taller than its surrounding neighbors.

If you've ever been to a city with tall skyscrapers, such as New York City, then you may well have noticed that from ground level all of the buildings appear to be roughly the same height. And yet if you ascend to a high level on one of the tallest buildings and look out, then you'll realize just how wrong your brain was.

In a similar way, your brain's analysis of the stacked rectangles to the right may tend to mislead you about their relative sizes. The smallest of the horizontal rectangles is in fact precisely the same size as the vertical rectangle.

In this row of brown columns, the gaps between the columns seem to get gradually wider. But do they?

Curved Conundrums

Which shape is bigger?

Your brain is excellent at making deductions even when given only small amounts of information to work from.

In the picture to the right, it applies information about relative location that it has learned from the real world and infers that the rightmost shape must be smaller than the leftmost one.

But as decoder E confirms, they are the same size.

Consider also the partially obscured circles below. Based on only what you can see, which circle do you think is the largest and which is the smallest?

In fact, all three circles are of identical size.

Central Questions

Which dot is in the exact center of each shape?

Where do you think the vertical center of the triangle to the right is?

It seems pretty obvious that it must be the middle dot—the other two are clearly some distance above or below the center point.

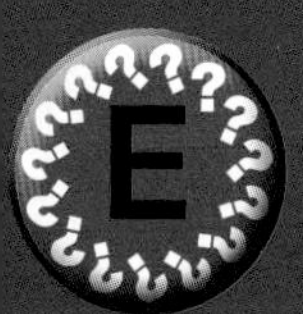

Use decoder E to find out if you're correct. The solution is on page 96.

In the heart to the left, which of the pink dots corresponds to the exact vertical center of the shape?

Once you've made your mind up, use decoder E and measure the distances in order to find out whether you were correct or not—or check on page 96.

A Lengthy Discussion

Do the line segments vary in length as they follow this wave?

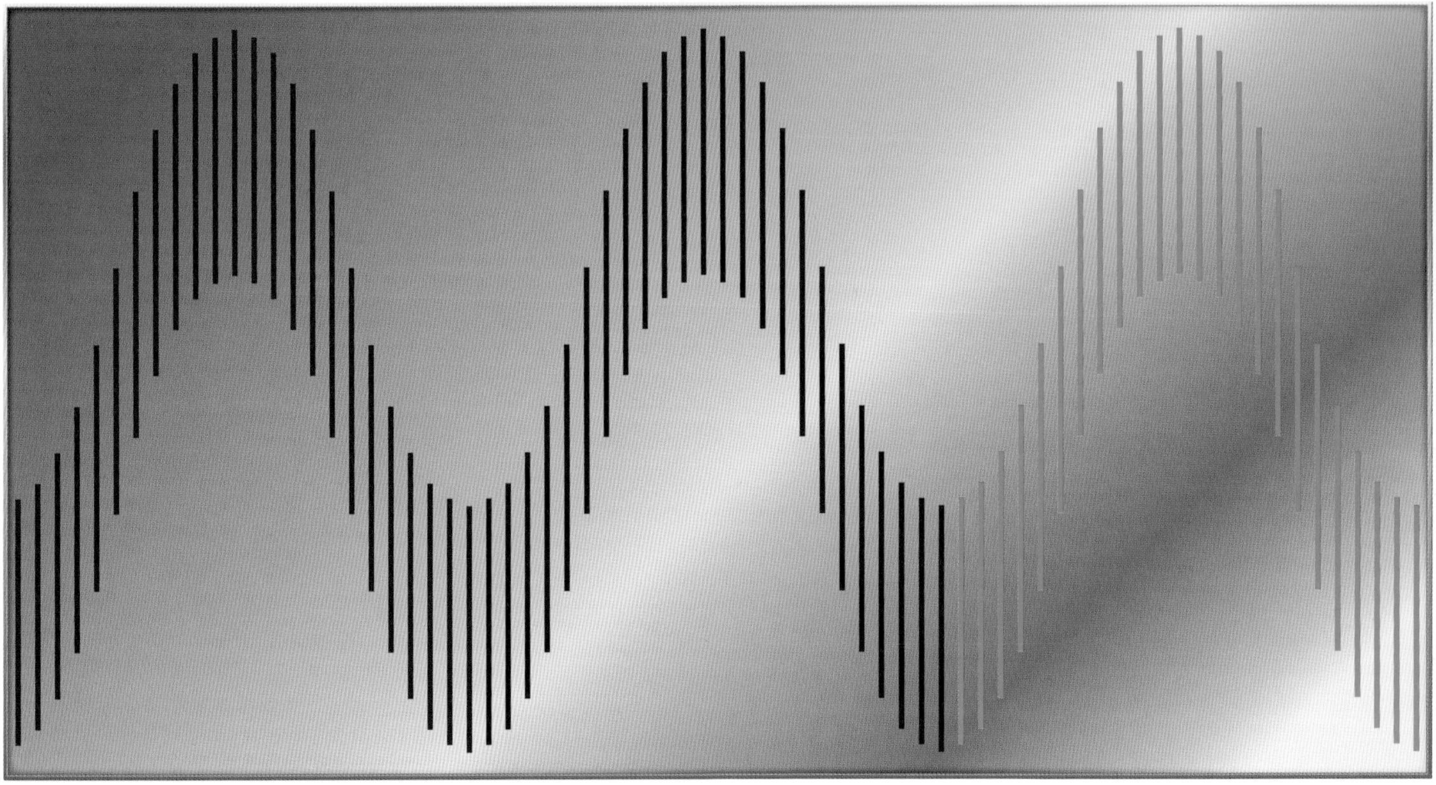

At first glance you probably assumed that the height of each bar varies with the distance from the vertical center of the wave, but as you can see when you look more closely—or use decoder E—the height is in fact constant throughout. This illusion works because the varying horizontal width of the wave leads your brain to assume that the height of each segment varies in sympathy with it. Or, in other words, larger areas are assumed to be made up of larger objects.

Is the distance between the left two points equal to that between the right two?

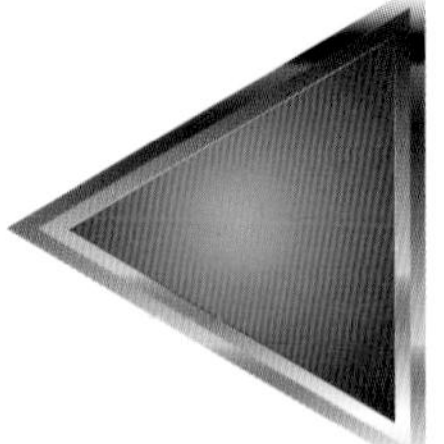

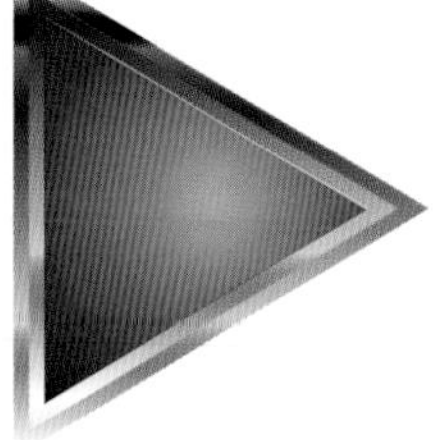

The distance from the point of the left triangle to the point of the center triangle appears to be much smaller than the distance between the points of the rightmost two triangles. But this is an illusion, similar to our inability to accurately find the center point of a triangle.

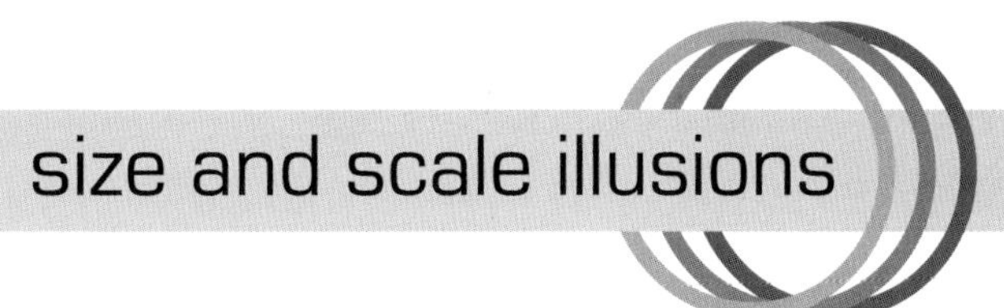

A Question of *Rotation*

Are these tabletop surfaces the same size? And the squares?

Take a good look at the tables to the right, and in particular at the tabletop surfaces.

Consider the width of the table to the right. Can you believe it is exactly the same as the length of the table below?

Not only that, but in fact the two tabletop shapes are absolutely identical in every way.

You can see a simpler version of this same illusion by looking at the squares below. The lower square appears larger, although they do in fact have identical dimensions.

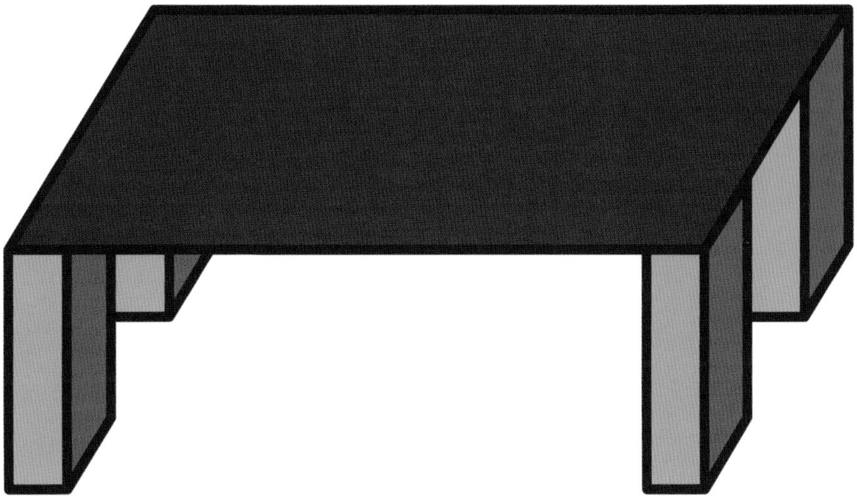

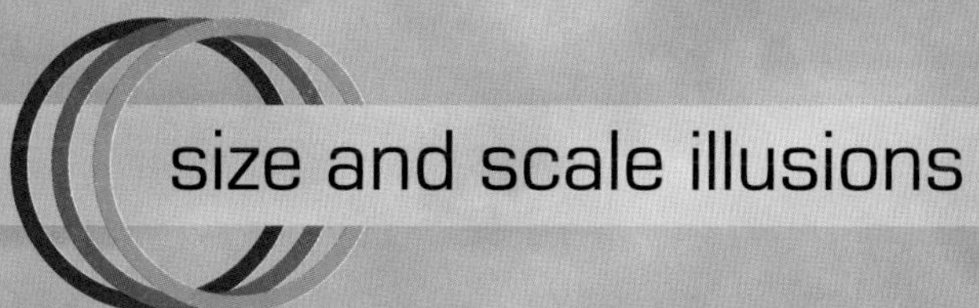

A Different View

If you close one eye, or take a photograph, then your sense of scale can get very confused.

Are these salt and pepper pots really different sizes?

Change the camera angle, and all is explained.

Alignment

Which colored line is a continuation of the white line?

Without rotating the book, imagine extending the white line further along its current route. When it reached the righthand side of the page, which of the colored lines would it overlap precisely?

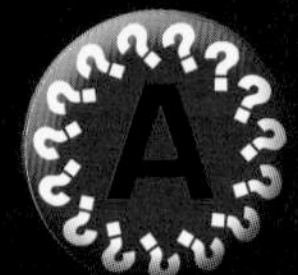

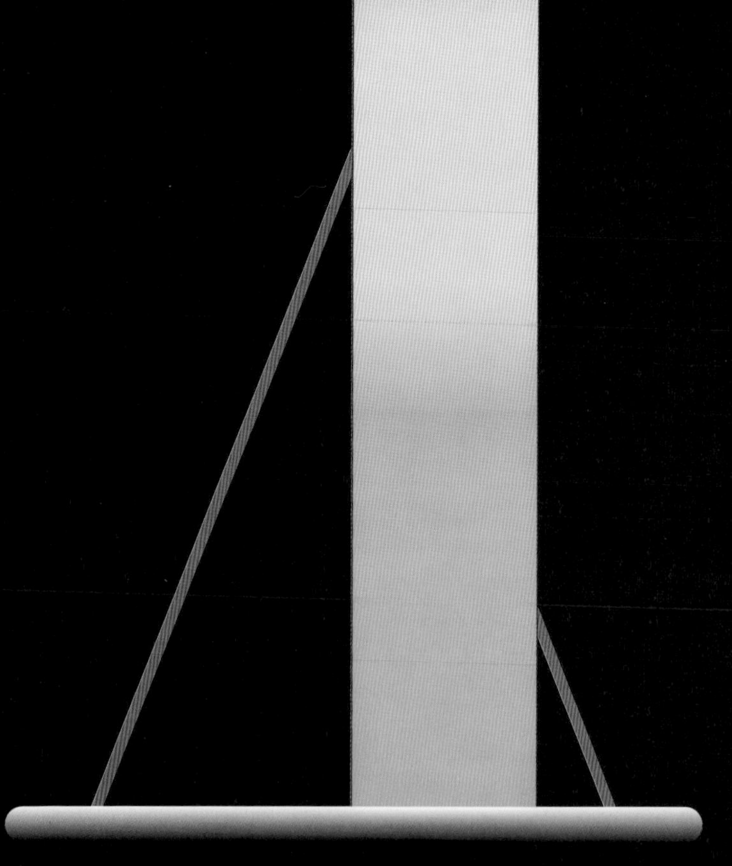

In the illusion to the right, the pink rods are partially hidden behind the orange rectangle.

It's hard to believe, but if you were to remove the orange obstruction, then the two pink lines would in fact meet and form a perfectly symmetric triangle.

The solution to the top illusion is the red line. Did you get it right?

Near and *Far*

Are the near and far objects the same size?

In the picture to the right, the narrowing of the strip and the increasing darkness as it appears to get "further away" encourage you to assume that the green circle at the back must be larger. They are actually exactly the same size.

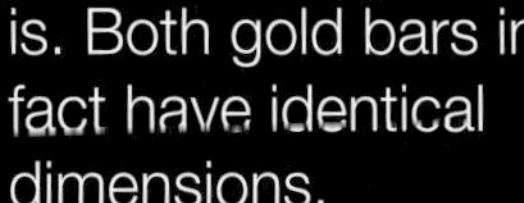

In the railway track illusion below, something similar is happening although the effect is even more powerful. The apparent increase in distance ensures our brains helpfully correct for distance, making the upper gold bar appear much larger than it actually is. Both gold bars in fact have identical dimensions.

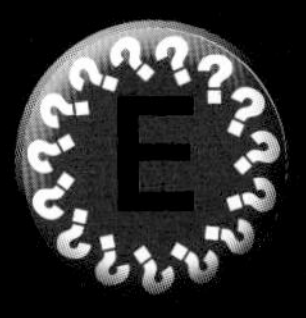

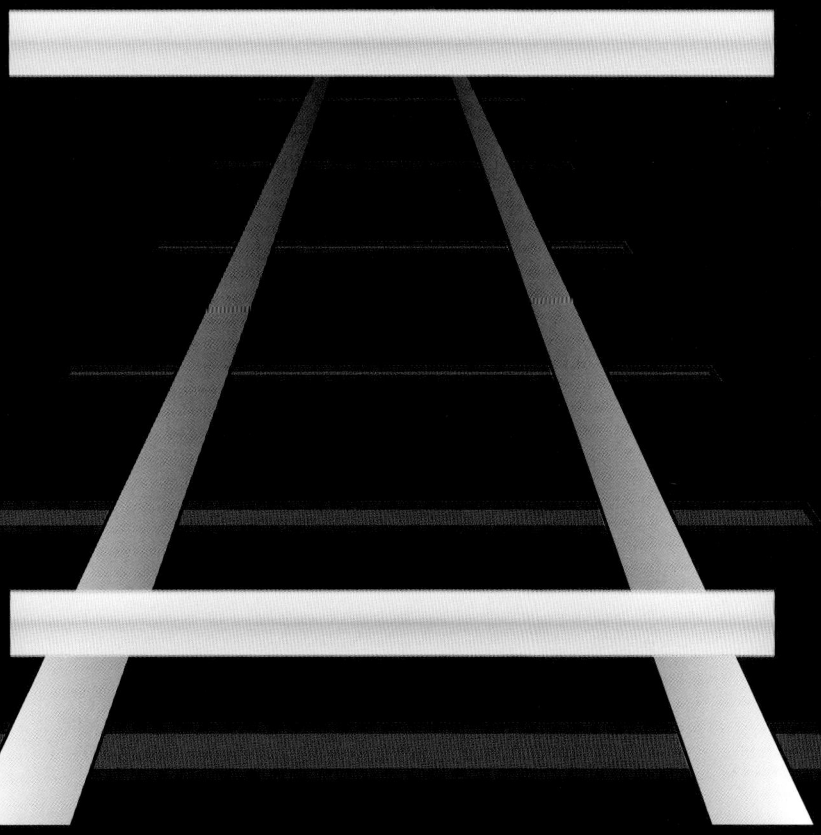

Leaning Towers

Does one of these towers lean further than the other?

The pictures are absolutely identical, so the lean is the same in both cases.

A Sense of **Direction**

Which path is straighter?

Again, both pictures are exactly the same so both are equally straight.

A Fresh *Perspective*

Changing your point of view needn't be just a conversational metaphor.

Place your eyes near the yellow circle and look in the direction of the arrow. Can you read the hidden text?

Now place one eye close to the bottom-left corner of this page and close the other eye. Look in the direction the lines tilt. You should be able to make all of the lines appear to rise vertically off the page in a surprisingly convincing 3D effect, although it may require a little experimentation to optimize the effect.

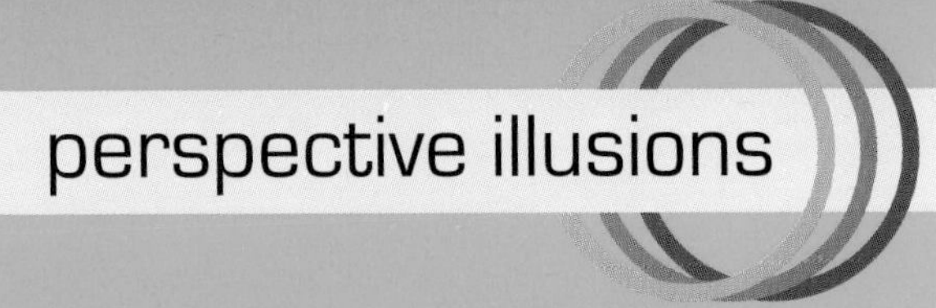

A *New* View

This appears to be an ordinary photograph, but can you spot the hidden pictures that it contains?

Fold a banknote along the eyes and nose of its portrait as shown in the top picture, resulting in the second picture. Now try tilting the banknote away from and then towards you. The portrait will frown or grin!

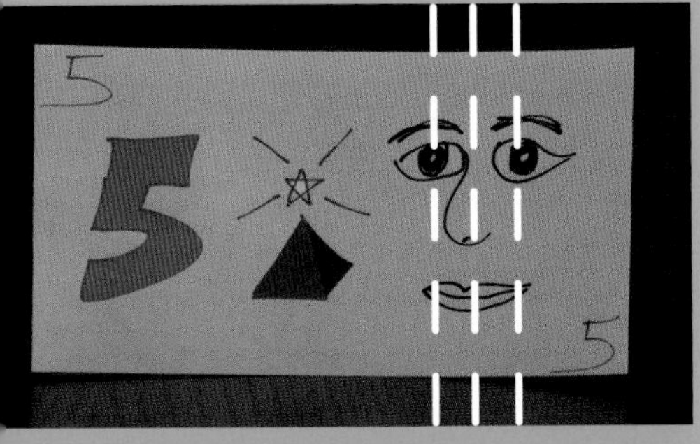

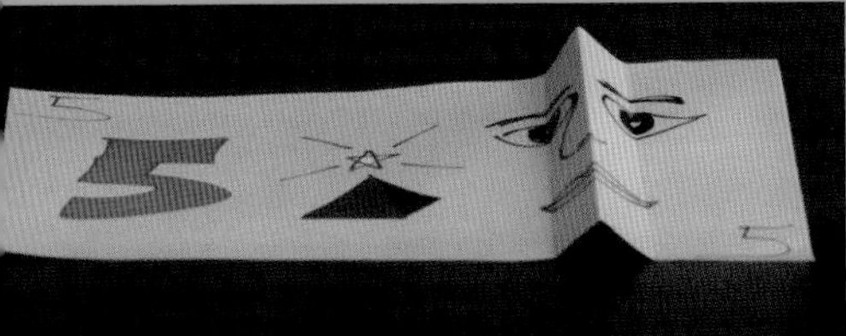

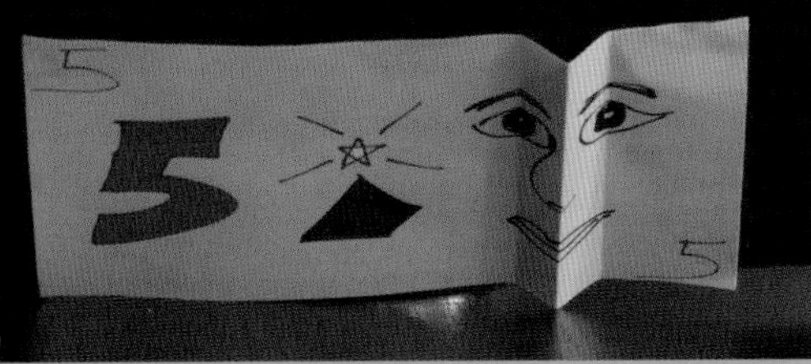

Hint: Hold the book parallel to the ground and look flat along the page. See page 96 for the solution.

The Power of **Suggestion**

Can you see four white shapes on this page? Or is your brain imagining them?

A Perception *of* Imperfection

Is this a perfect hexagon?

The brain is fantastic at spotting patterns and making deductions based on the limited information it has, as the apparently white shapes on the opposite page demonstrate.

But, in the picture to the left, the purple triangles, despite obscuring only a small proportion of the hexagon, convince the eye that the underlying shape is irregular. It is, in fact, a regular and perfectly symmetric hexagon.

Is this a perfect circle?

Gravity doesn't just affect physical objects—the presence of nearby objects also changes our perceptions of adjacent shapes.

Although the effect is relatively weak, in the illustration to the right the disk shape appears to protrude slightly at the places adjacent to the prongs.

It is actually a perfect circle, and it is just an optical illusion.

Shape **Perception**

How many circles do you see?

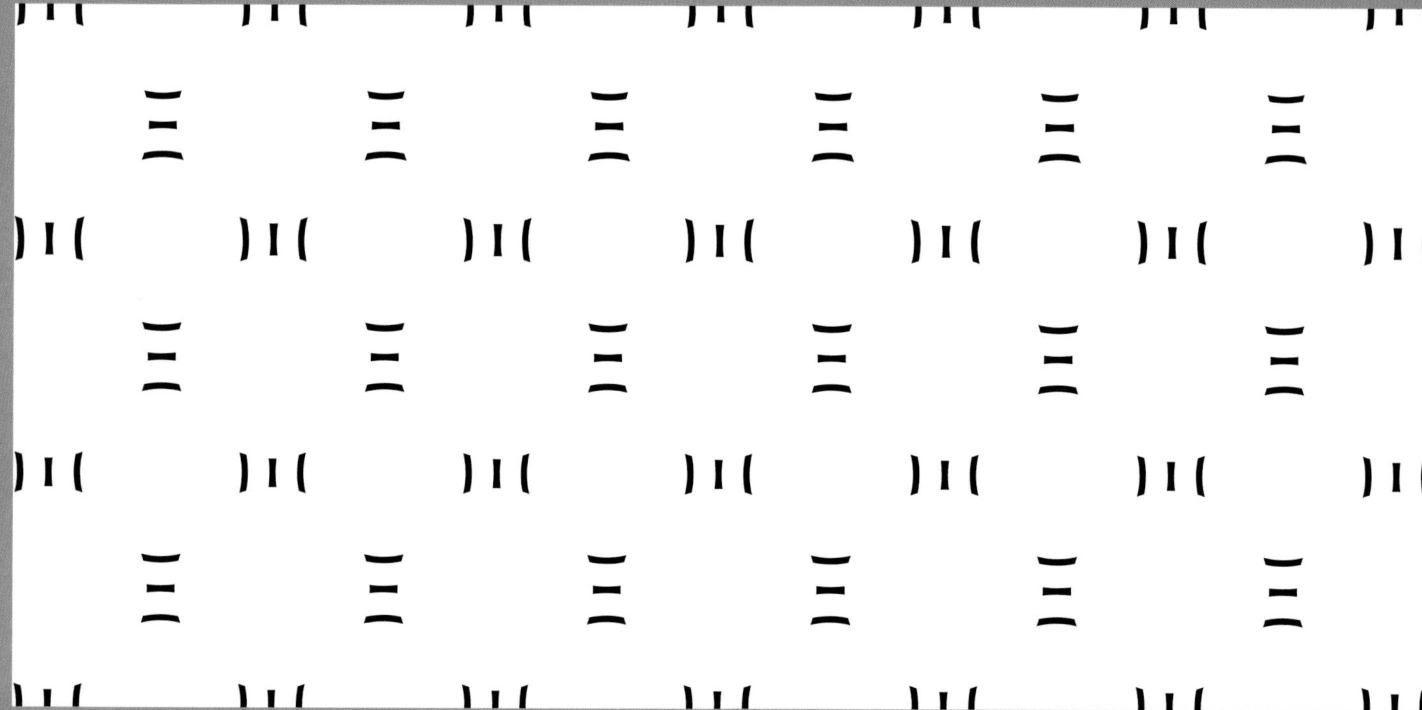

Just the merest suggestion of a circle is enough for the brain to deduce their presence, as the picture above shows. This diagram contains two types of circle—smaller ones which are shown only by the tiny parts of concave arc, and larger ones contained in the gaps between the ends of those arcs. Given so little information it's remarkable that you can still see these predominantly white-on-white circles so well!

The diagram to the right demonstrates an entirely different effect. This time it appears to be a grid of fully drawn circles, and indeed that's exactly what it is. But put this book down, step back several paces and look again. The chances are that each white circle will look like a white hexagon!

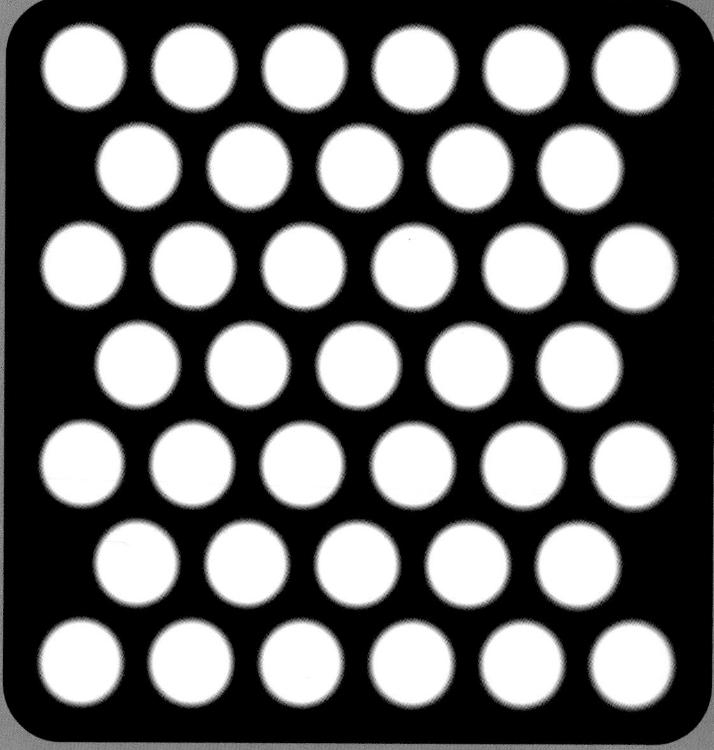

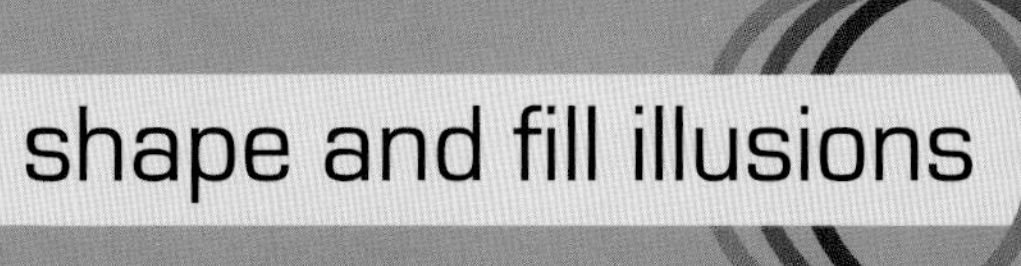

Straight-line *Curves*

Do you see a grid of straight lines or an arrangement of white circles?

In this remarkable illusion, crosses and straight lines imply bright white circles. Only straight lines with flat end caps have been used to draw this image, and yet the impression left is not of a pattern of lines but rather a grid of glowing, whiter-than-paper disks.

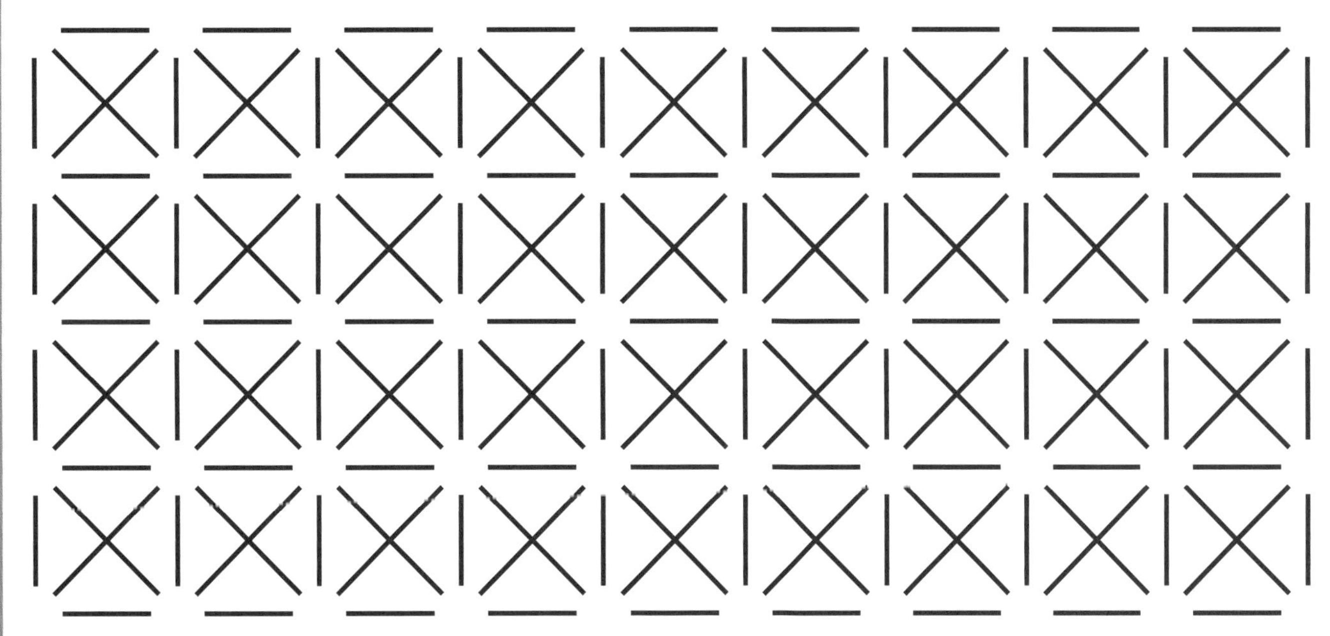

Even more remarkably, you still see the circles even when the diagonal lines are removed.

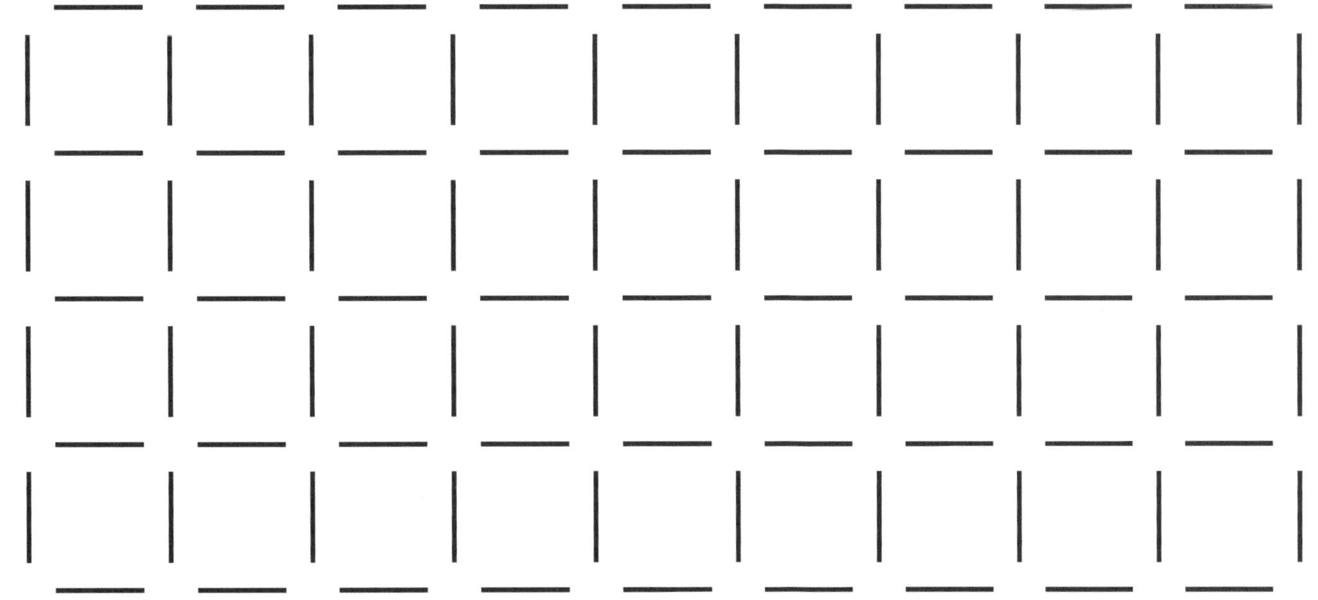

Moiré and More

Can you see the swirling, eddying patterns that these simple curves produce?

A *Focus* on Focus

Do you find it difficult to fix your eyes on these confusing patterns?

A moiré pattern is an interference pattern created by overlapping two different sets of lines and, as these pages show, these effects can be strong even when using relatively simple arrangements of lines.

Moving the page can help accent these effects. Try moving the book away from you and towards you while looking at the center of one of the swirls.

On the grid of squares below, your eyes find it remarkably hard to decide where to look—there is nothing for them to focus on and so they wander around chaotically. This even happens when you deliberately try to concentrate on a particular square. You might also try angling the page away from you and looking at the grid.

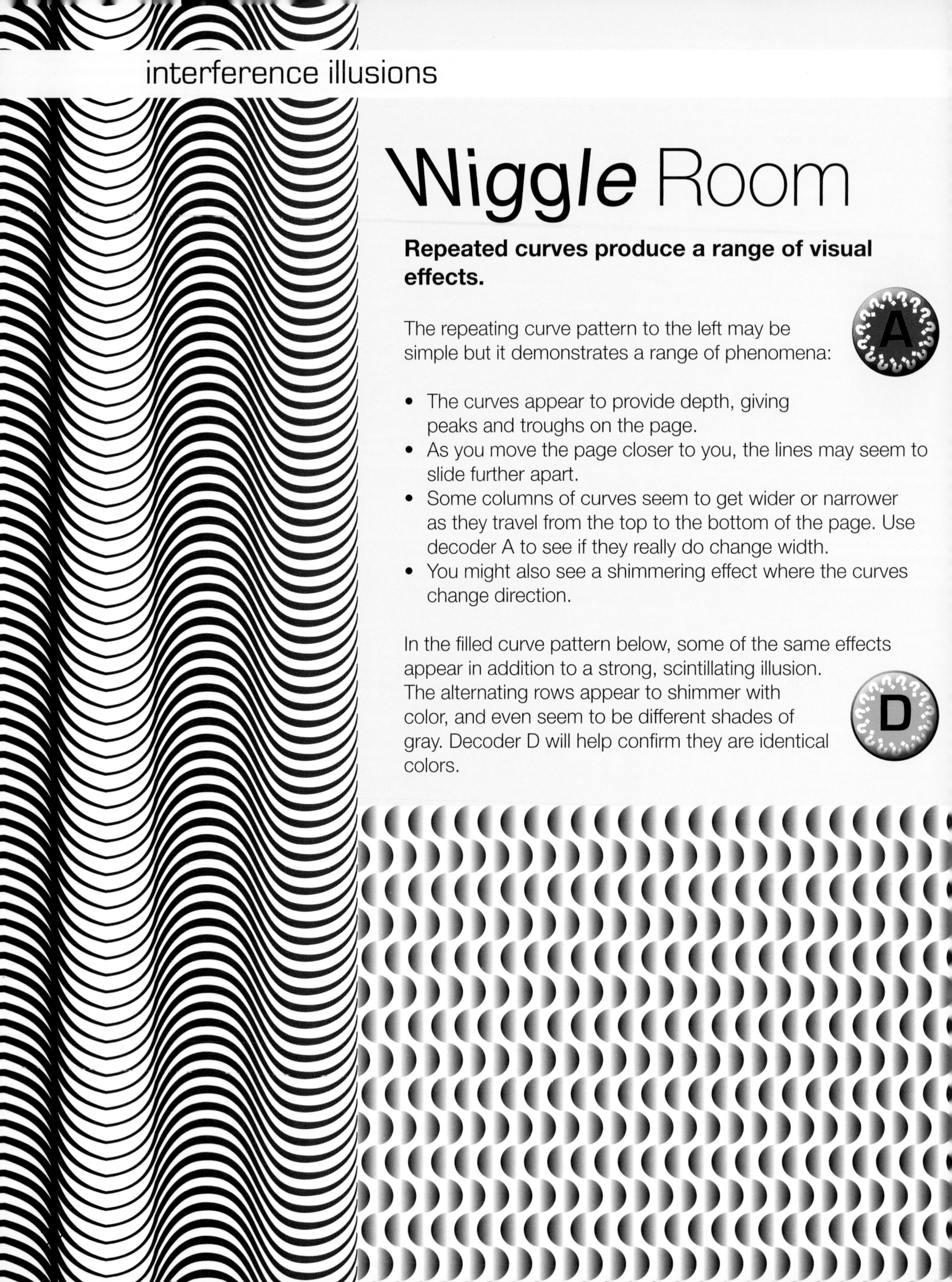

Wiggle Room

Repeated curves produce a range of visual effects.

The repeating curve pattern to the left may be simple but it demonstrates a range of phenomena:

- The curves appear to provide depth, giving peaks and troughs on the page.
- As you move the page closer to you, the lines may seem to slide further apart.
- Some columns of curves seem to get wider or narrower as they travel from the top to the bottom of the page. Use decoder A to see if they really do change width.
- You might also see a shimmering effect where the curves change direction.

In the filled curve pattern below, some of the same effects appear in addition to a strong, scintillating illusion. The alternating rows appear to shimmer with color, and even seem to be different shades of gray. Decoder D will help confirm they are identical colors.

Circular Confusion

Do the wavy lines in this circular arrangement induce a range of motion and shimmering patterns as you move the book towards and then away from you?

Warp In

Does the pattern seem to spiral in towards the center?

You can see that this pattern is constructed of four concentric circles, none of which overlap at all. And yet, despite this observation, it's still easy to perceive the squares as forming a continuous spiral emanating from the center, especially if you let your eyes wander around the picture.

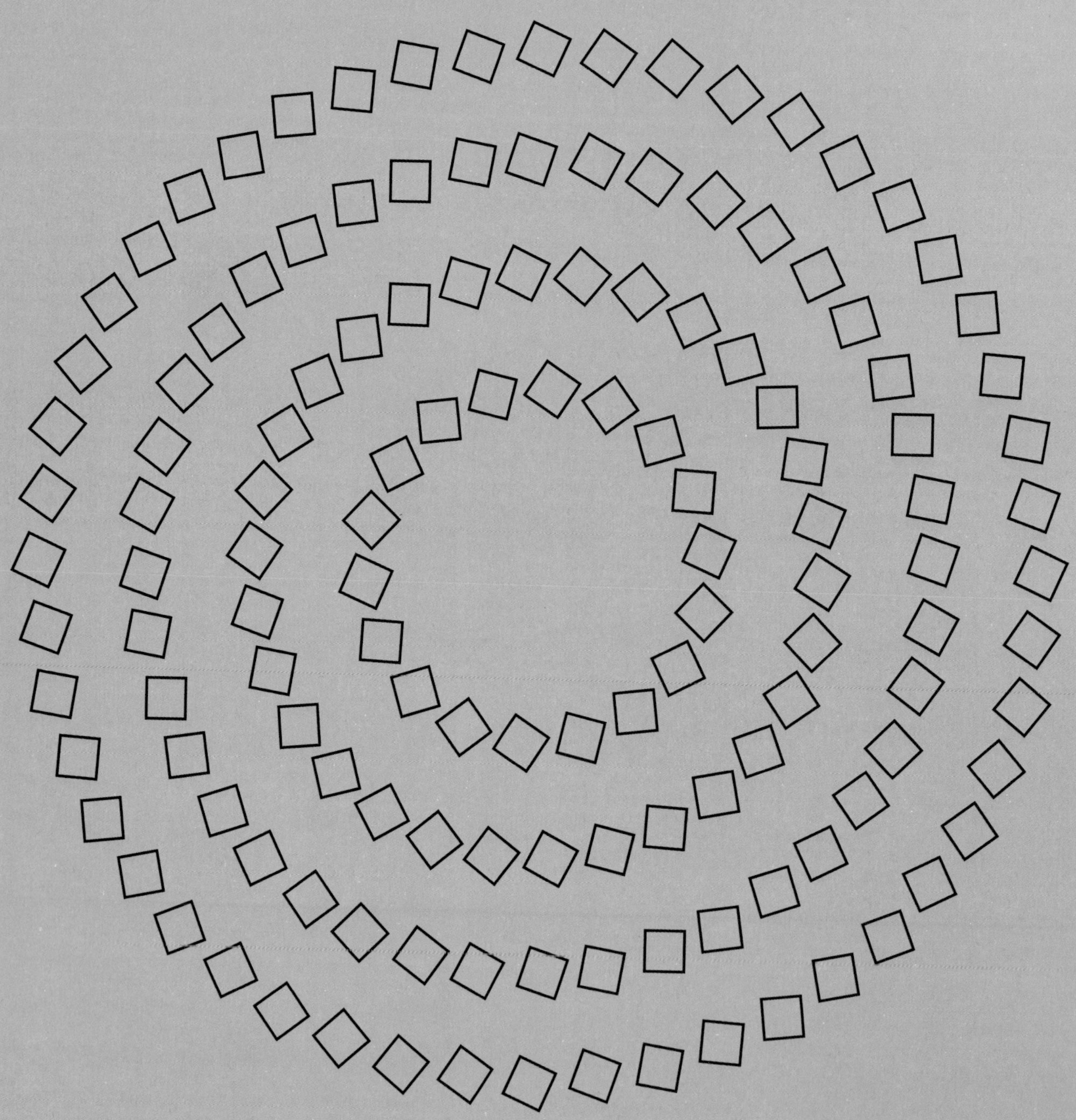

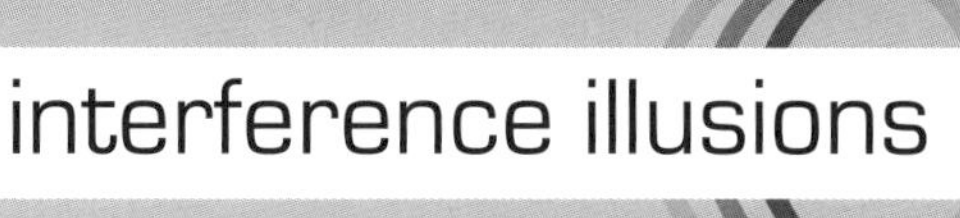

Warp Out

Is this a spiral pulling you into a central hole?

The grooves in this pattern appear to twist in towards the middle of the picture, forming an even more explicit spiral than the illusion on the opposite page. Yet these are, in fact, perfect circles.

Shimmering **Vision**

Move your eyes around the picture. What color are the dots?

Unless you hold the book extremely close or ridiculously far away, it's impossible to look at the dots in this illustration without seeing lots of shimmering dark spots on neighboring intersections. There is no definitive scientific explanation for why this strong, scintillating effect occurs.

Ghosts

Let your eyes wander around the yellow grid. Do you see faint yellow dots?

If you stare at a particular gap between the squares then you can easily see that it is the same solid black as the background color. But move your eyes across to a neighbor and the ghostly yellow dots creep back.

Decoder B will help confirm that they are just imaginary.

What do you see as you move your eyes over these daisy patterns?

These flowers shimmer vividly as you move your eyes around them. You may also find that holding the book closer to your eyes increases the strength of the effect.

As in the illusions above and opposite, if you look directly at a flower it may stabilize. But as soon as you look away the ghostly patterns begin all over again.

Alignment Issues

Do these patterns appear to be sliding around?

Move your eyes slowly left and right, following the blue squares in the picture below. As you move across, so entire columns appear to be sliding up and down, in a desperate attempt at visual alignment.

As you run your eyes up and down this image the diagonal lines below appear to slide left and right, and as they do so you may also see ghostly patterns running back and forth along the yellow bars.

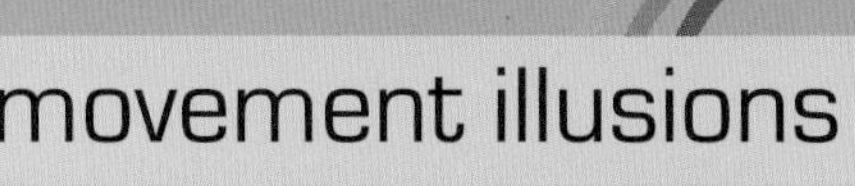

Floating Around

Hold the book a little closer and then look around each image.

The "raft" in the center of the top-right image appears to float in front of the sea of blurred posts. The separation from the background that you see can be quite uncanny.

The pattern at the bottom left swirls left and right in a tidal flow of shifting columns. The effect is strongest if you move your eyes slowly from dot to dot while the illusion fills a good proportion of your field of vision.

The illusion at the bottom right is similar to its neighbor, except that the movement is far more chaotic and shifts not just left and right but up and down as well.

All three of these illusions are based on simulating shadow or highlight effects which the brain uses to calculate both depth and relative position.

Passing in a **Blur**

Look at the circle and slowly move the book closer to you.

Do you see smears streaking by, like stars in a sci-fi movie?

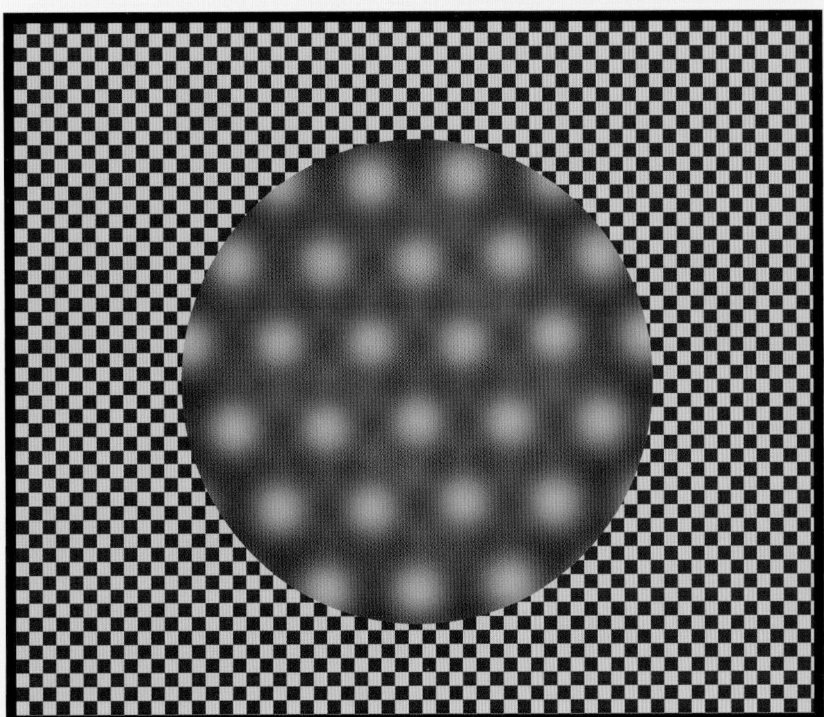

Blurred Out

Relax your eyes on the blurred circle in the image above. Does it separate from the background?

Your brain may be confused by the strong contrast between the pin-sharp background and the blurred foreground, giving an impression of separation between levels.

When you hold the book at arm's length, does the image to the right shimmer?

In this picture neither of the two layers are blurred, but the contrast in colors is so great that you may still see a shimmering movement at the place where the diamond shapes touch.

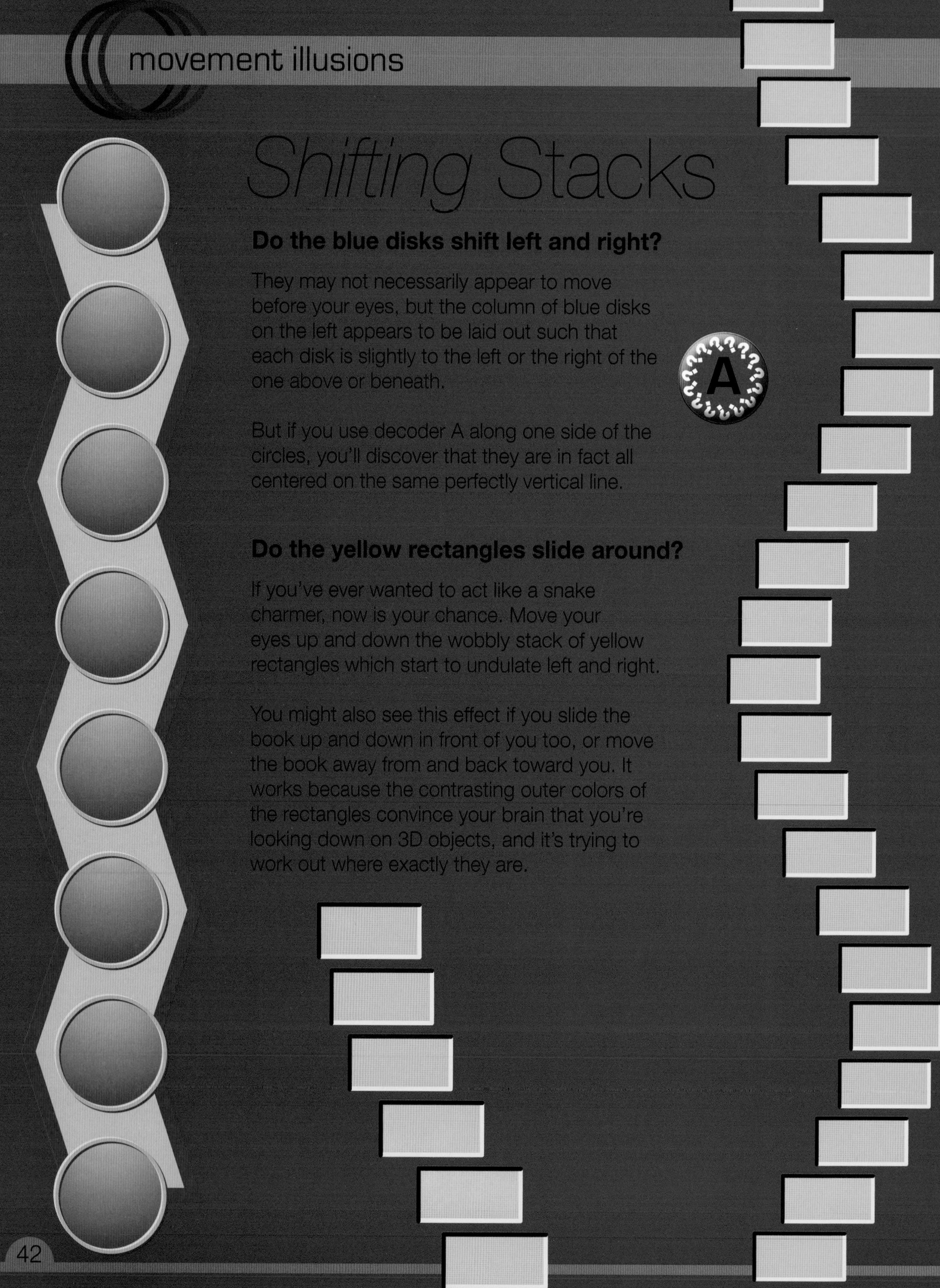

Shifting Stacks

Do the blue disks shift left and right?

They may not necessarily appear to move before your eyes, but the column of blue disks on the left appears to be laid out such that each disk is slightly to the left or the right of the one above or beneath.

But if you use decoder A along one side of the circles, you'll discover that they are in fact all centered on the same perfectly vertical line.

Do the yellow rectangles slide around?

If you've ever wanted to act like a snake charmer, now is your chance. Move your eyes up and down the wobbly stack of yellow rectangles which start to undulate left and right.

You might also see this effect if you slide the book up and down in front of you too, or move the book away from and back toward you. It works because the contrasting outer colors of the rectangles convince your brain that you're looking down on 3D objects, and it's trying to work out where exactly they are.

Take a **Closer** Look

Look at the central blue disk and slowly move it closer. Do the rings move too?

Moving *the* Immovable

Watch the center of this picture while slowly shaking the book left and right or up and down.

As you move the book, does the circle appear to float on top of the background? If you don't see this straight away, hold the page at arm's length and try again. Now rotate the book 90 degrees and repeat the exercise. The circle now sinks *behind* the page.

To the right is a pattern of tiled circles. Up close there's nothing else to see, but move the book further away from you and a hidden square will be revealed.

Then try moving the image back and forth. The square separates from its background.

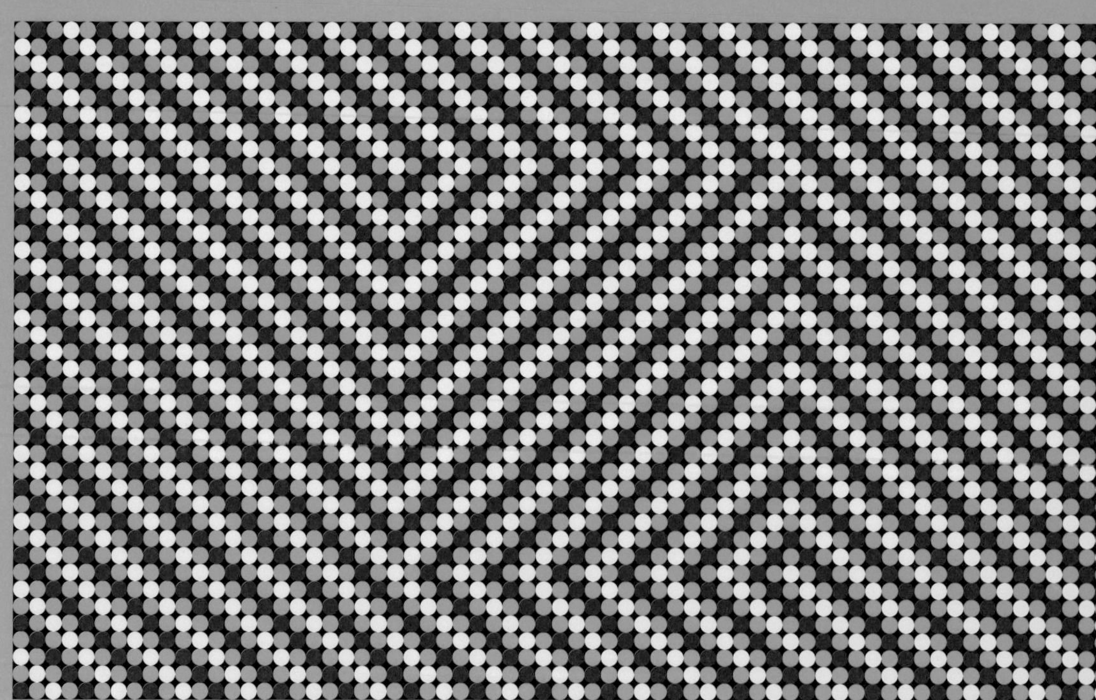

Round *and* **Round**

Focus on the dot in the center and then slowly move the book closer to you.

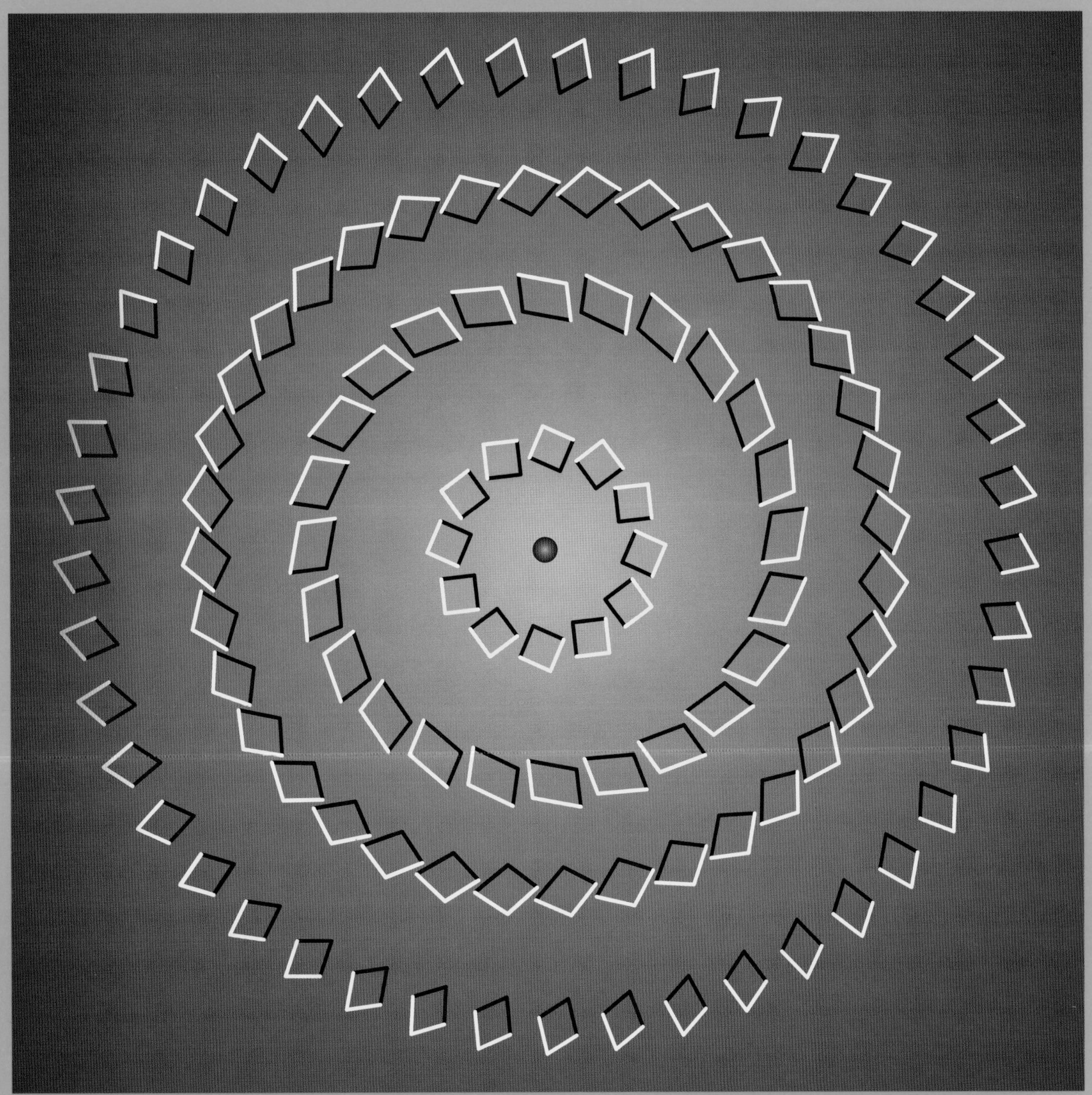

The rings appear to rotate in opposing directions, and these reverse when you move the book away from you. You might also see them as a stacked set of rotating disks.

Orientation Assumptions

What shapes do you see to the left?

The chances are that because these squares are all in a row that you don't have much trouble observing them as just that: squares. But what if they were tipped on their side, like those below?

What do you see here? It seems pretty obvious that these are diamonds, even though they are absolutely identical and they're even at the same orientation. There really is nothing different about the shapes at all.

This demonstrates how important context is to the brain's interpretation of what it sees.

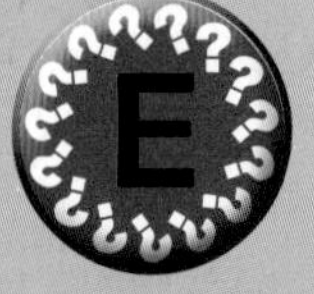

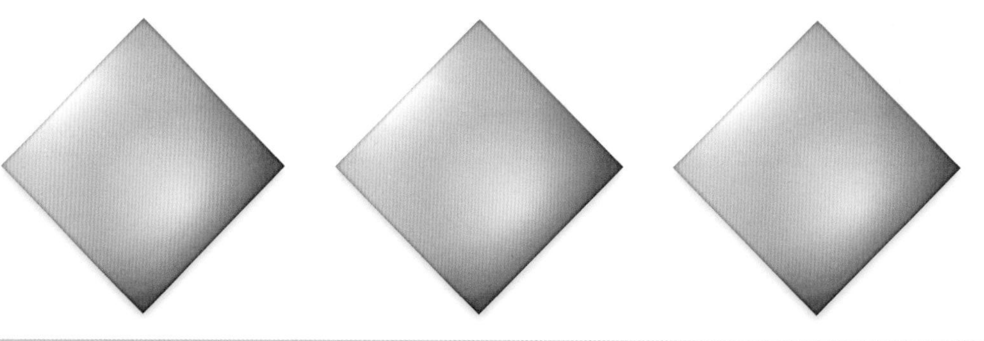

The angular pattern on the right is another example of how the brain makes orientation assumptions based on context. Although these are simple repeated lines, you probably have no trouble seeing them as rows of benches. In fact, you might even see the "seated" areas as a different color from the vertical back parts.

Cubes, Cubes, Cubes

Can you see 3D cubes in even the simplest wireframes?

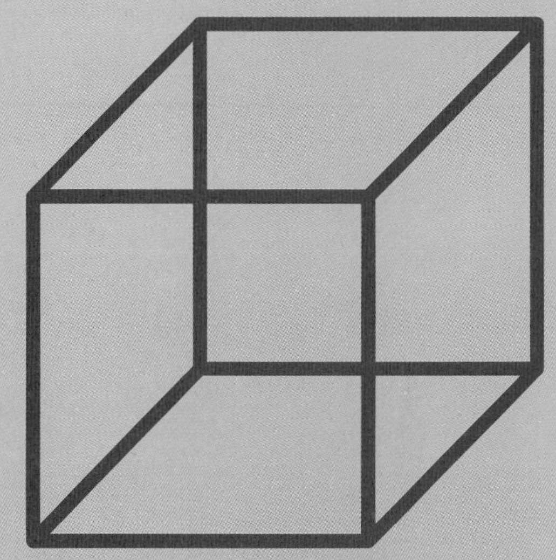

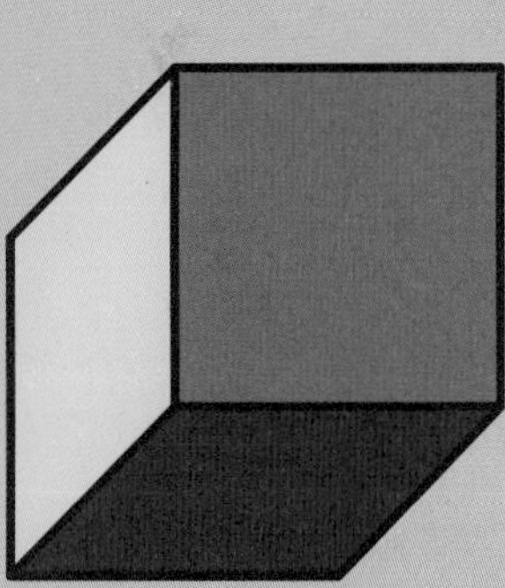

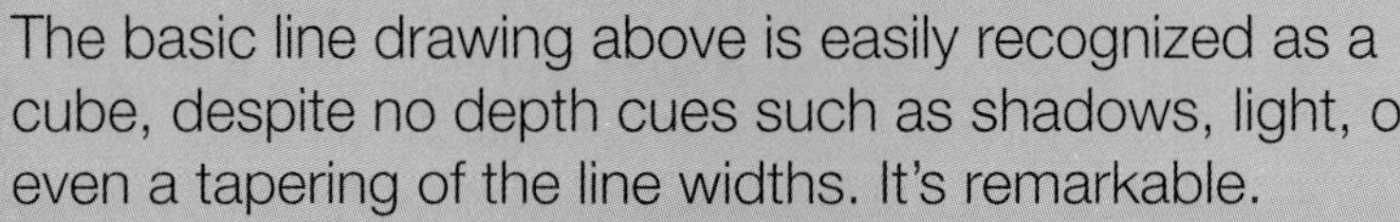

The basic line drawing above is easily recognized as a cube, despite no depth cues such as shadows, light, or even a tapering of the line widths. It's remarkable.

When cubes are viewed like this, however, it isn't clear which way the cube actually "points"—is the square at the top right of this cube pointing out of the book, or is the square at the bottom left pointing out? You might find it hard to see the alternative explanation to whichever you spotted first, but keep trying and suddenly it will "pop" into the opposing orientation.

In the set of four shaded cubes, the shading creates a different orientation confusion. For each drawing, is it a cube or is it a view of the interior of a room? Again, whichever you saw first can be hard to overrule with the alternative interpretation. Your brain also makes assumptions based on common lighting patterns, so even though all four cubes are identical and merely rotated 90, 180 or 270 degrees, you may well find that you see some of them as rooms and others as cubes.

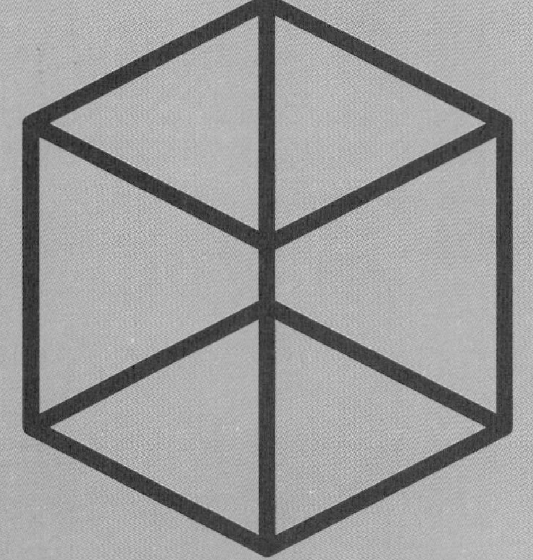

In fact, surprisingly little information is needed to identify a cube. Consider the hexagonal wireframe to the left. This is still clearly a cube. Even the perfectly symmetrical hexagon to the right can easily be seen as a cube.

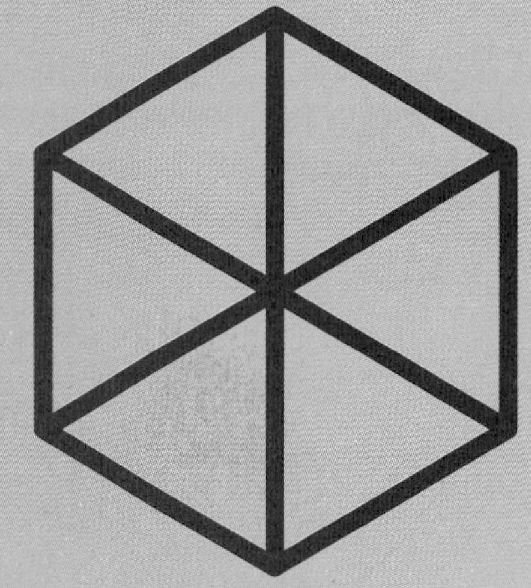

A Point of View

Which way is this chair facing?

Depending upon how you initially look at this chair, you may see it as either facing the wall or facing out into the room. Whichever you notice first, look at the right-hand part of the chair back until it "pops" into the other position.

This illusion works because the chair has been converted to almost complete shadow, and there is not enough variation in the width of the vertical struts to otherwise disambiguate. The rear shadow is also ambiguous, given the point of view. The rear struts have been straightened and the tops of the backs leveled, to remove any perspective cues.

Which Way Up?

Which way do the cylinders point?

In this illustration the cylinders will "flip-flop" their direction as you look at them. They can be seen in two ways, so that either the bottom part appears to be inside the tube or alternatively it can appear to be outside the tube. You might find it hard to see the alternative view to whichever you see first, but persevere.

The image to the left also appears to be one of two things, depending on whichever you see first. It is either a picture of the blank interior of a book or, alternatively, it is a book facing away from you with a blank cover.

Both views are entirely valid, but again whichever you see first will tend to stick with you until you force your brain to consider the alternative.

This also works with the simple pictorial representation below.

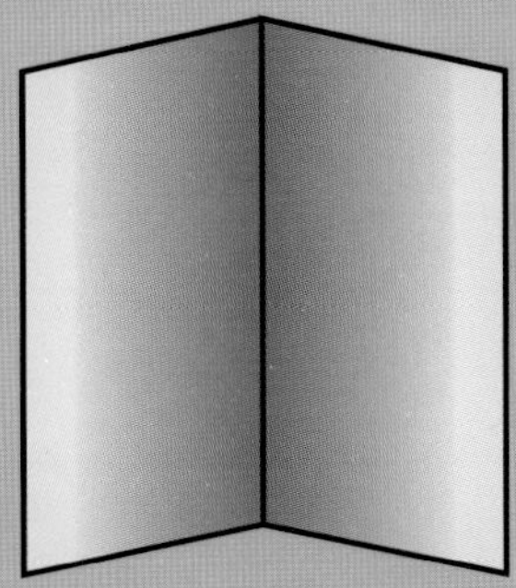

Shadow *Power*

Which spoon is facing up? And which sphere is furthest up the page?

We make a lot of assumptions based on how the sun lights the world, even though with so many sources of electric light this may not always be accurate. Consider the spoon in the left picture. Is the scoop side facing you or is it facing away? And what about the right-hand picture? The photograph is identical except that the bowl part has been edited to rotate it 180 degrees. Does this affect your perception?

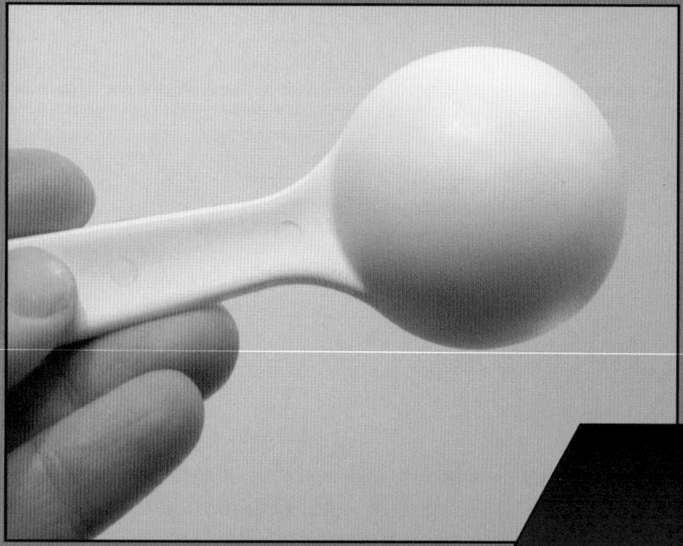

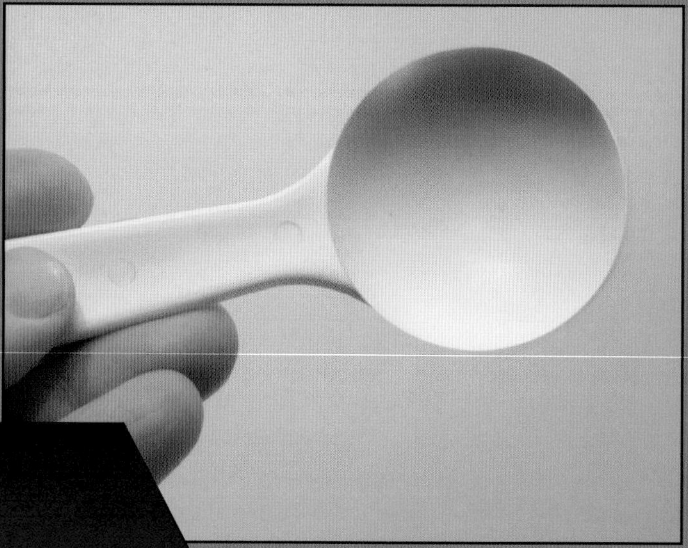

Since shadows tell us about depth, which is critical to navigating the world, they provide powerful information that it is very hard to ignore.

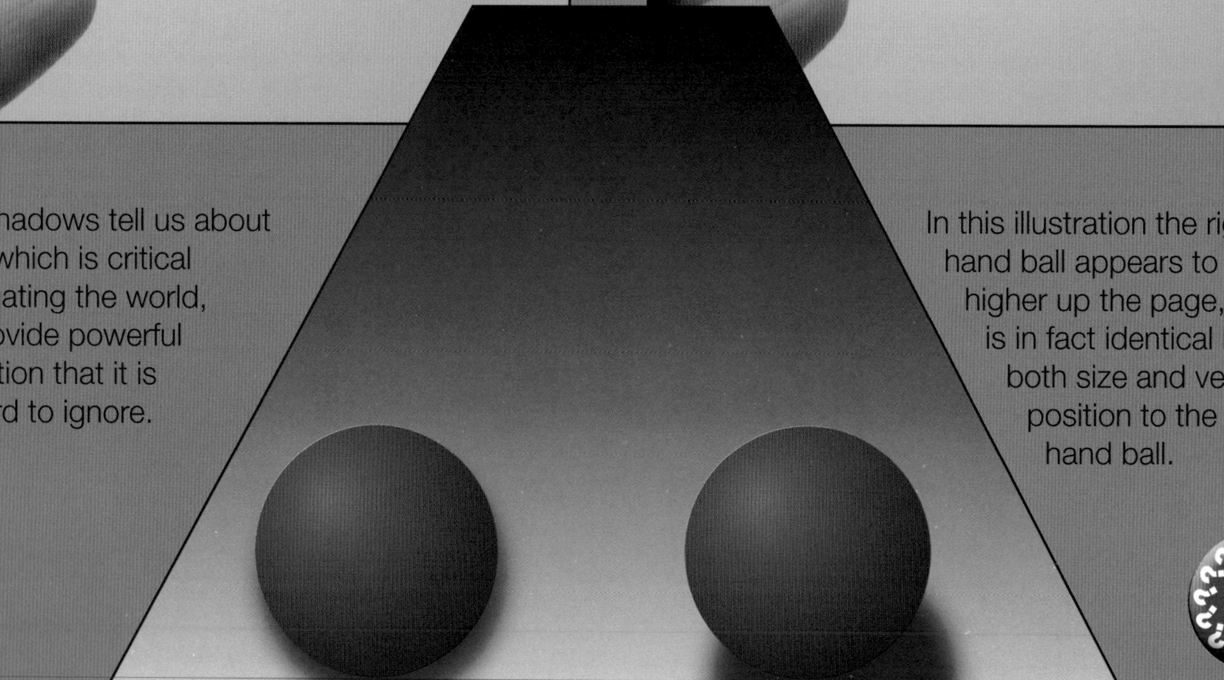

In this illustration the right-hand ball appears to be higher up the page, but is in fact identical in both size and vertical position to the left-hand ball.

A

Visual *Confusion*

Can you find the star in the line drawing?

It's possible to confuse the brain. Despite its great skill at pattern-spotting, even simple camouflage patterns can be astonishingly effective. Consider, for example, the star to the right. It seems very unlikely that this could be well camouflaged with just a few extra lines, and yet consider the image at the bottom of this page.

A complete star is hidden in the illustration below, identical in shape—but not necessarily size or orientation—to the red star to the right. Can you find it?

If you give up, the solution is on page 96—it's surprisingly hard to spot!

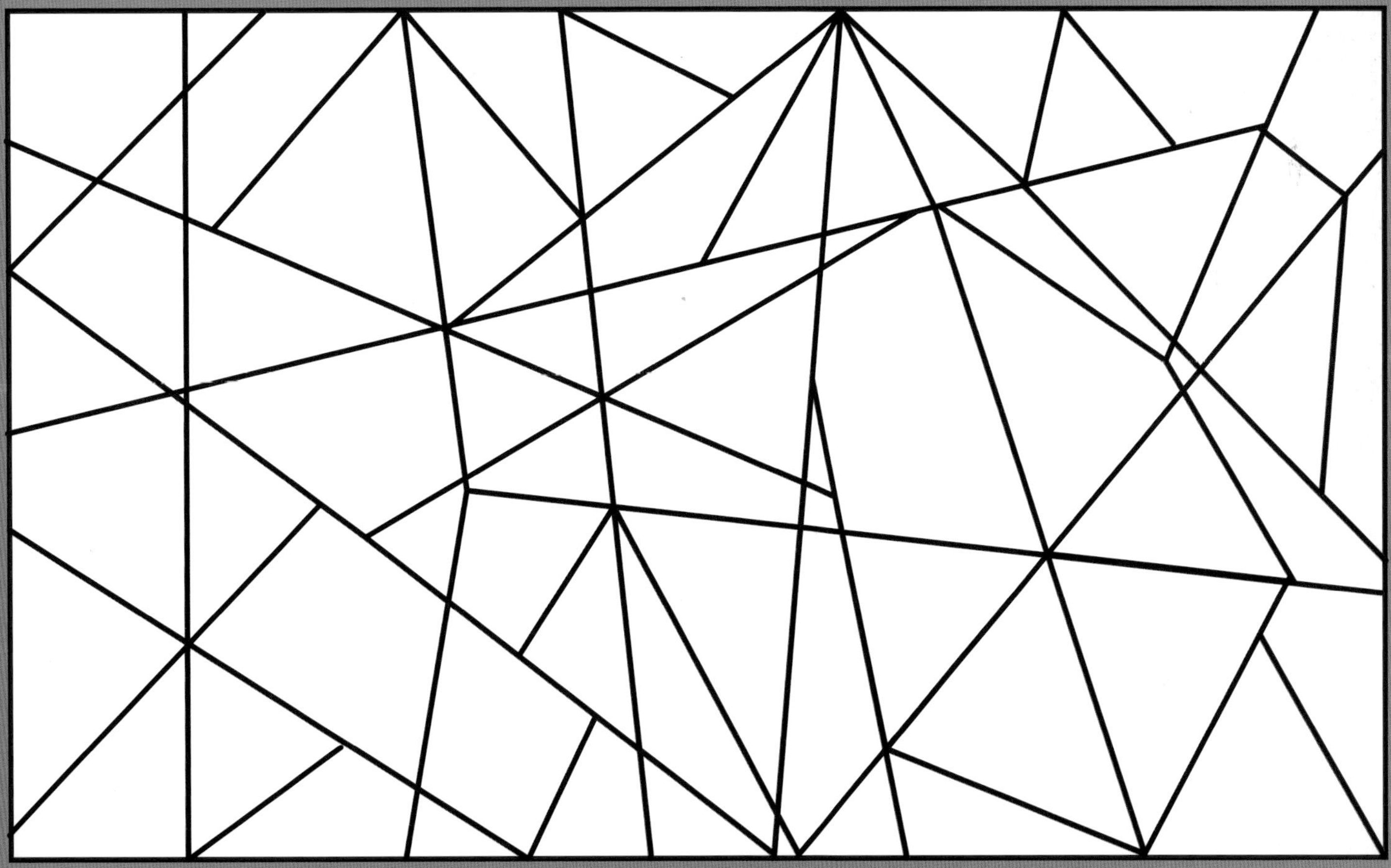

Impossible Objects

What's wrong with these pictures?

Context is a key clue to the brain for disambiguating objects and working out what's important and what isn't, but it can also be used to mislead.

Focus your attention on just one of the three corners of the green triangular shape. Looking just at that local area, it seems reasonable that such a shape could exist. Yet if you take a step back and look at the whole picture it becomes apparent that no such shape could actually be constructed.

Taken in a local context the image is fine, so it takes conscious thought to work out that the shape isn't valid.

Consider also the blue rectangle below. Because this is wider, it's even harder to associate the context of one side with that of the other, so this object almost looks like it could be real.

Perhaps you could replace a mailbox slot with this, to confuse the delivery person?

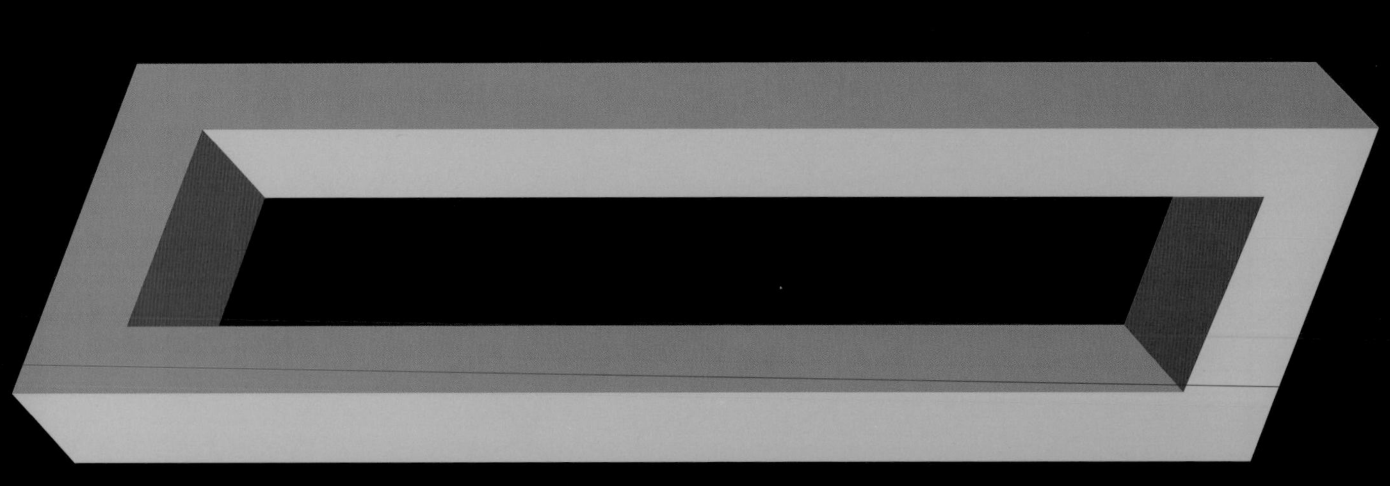

Impossible *arrangements*

What's wrong with these various assemblies?

It's possible to assemble perfectly sensible objects into impossible arrangements, or at least it is when you're drawing them rather than trying to build them!

As you can see, it wouldn't be possible to build any of the structures on this page. They're all based on cubes, but none of them could be built with real ones.

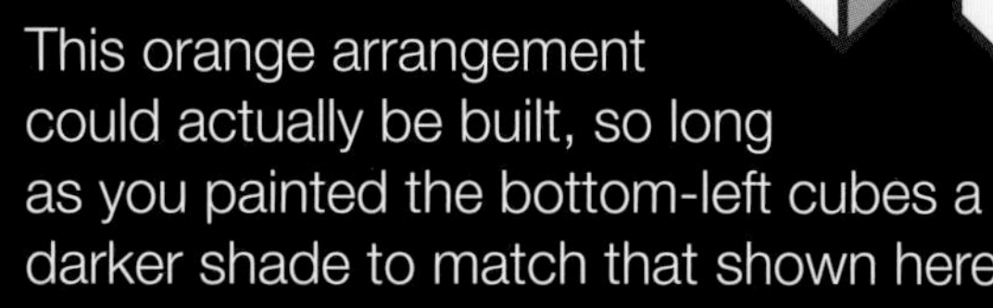

This orange arrangement could actually be built, so long as you painted the bottom-left cubes a darker shade to match that shown here!

Stack 'em Up

Can you recreate this photograph using just twelve dice?

Superficially, the answer is no—the arrangement is impossible because the top-right and top-left dice are floating in mid-air.

But in fact it would be possible to arrange the dice to look like this purely for the purposes of a photograph, by placing the two extra dice on the table further back behind the front stack and then taking the picture from a carefully chosen angle.

Fitting the Picture

Can you join the dots to make a perfect square?

The red dots to the left appear to be haphazardly arranged in a rough circle—and to some extent indeed they are. But they are also all sitting exactly on the edge of a square.

Can you work out where the square is, so that the edges of the square run through each dot?

Impossible? Not at all. Given that it is solvable it should surely be easy, and yet the chances are that you'll find this task takes more than a moment's thought!

Superficially these tables make sense, but there's something very strange going on with the surface they're sitting on. Can you explain exactly what that is?

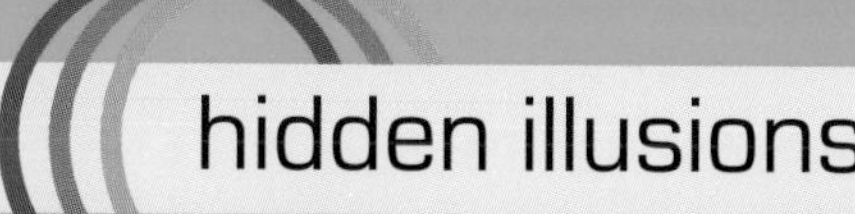

Good/Bad For Your Eyes

Do you see a pastoral sunset?

If something is more-or-less as the brain expects it to be, then it's quite happy to tick it off as "successfully observed" and move on to other things.

You probably spotted very quickly that the sun in the image below has been replaced with a slice of carrot, but was it the very first thing you thought the moment you turned the page? It probably took you a moment to notice, no matter how brief that moment was. Staring into the sun isn't good for your eyes, but ironically carrots are!

Always Eat Your Greens

Unless they're mutant?

If you've read the opposite page then you're primed to look for something unusual here; but even so at a casual glance the greenery on this page looks uniform enough that your very first thought on processing this image is not to look out for mutant greens, but instead to take it in as a gentle seascape.

The broccoli is somewhat treelike, but once you spot that it's broccoli there's no forgetting it—you can't mistake it for a tree a second time!

INVERSE images

There is something special about this grumpy man. Can you make him smile?

Just as the gaps between the left-pointing white arrows at the top of this page create the image of additional black arrows pointing to the right, or the reverse on the opposite page, so too this man has an opposing alternative interpretation.

Turn the book upside down and the grumpy man becomes much happier! His beard becomes the top of his head, and his bushy eyebrows become a mustache.

Even the simplest sketches can transform in surprising ways. Consider the cheeky fellow below. Turn him upside down—do you see a cute baby in a baseball cap? Can you draw your own?

inverse **IMAGES**

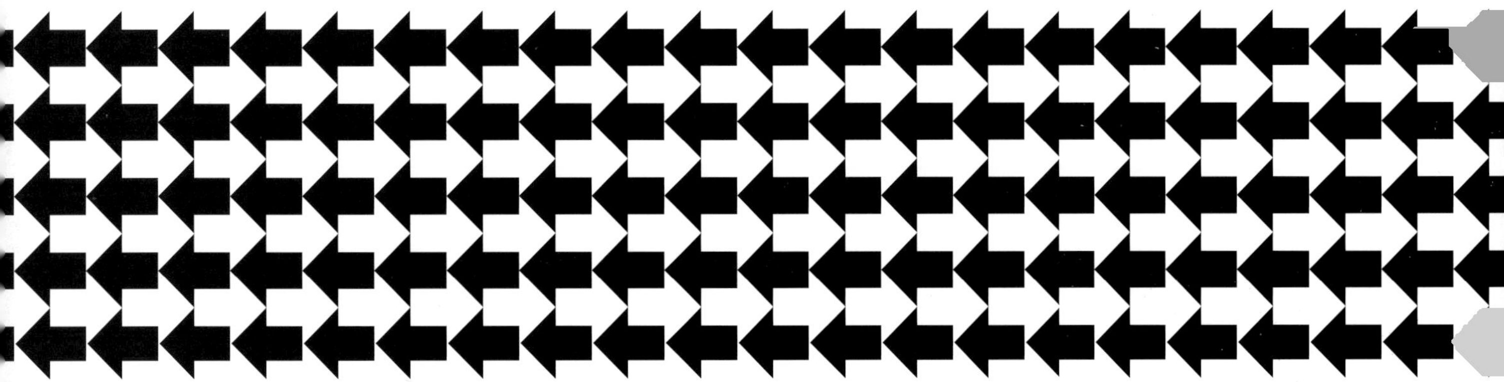

Sheep are happily grazing on these hills. But can you turn them into mountains?

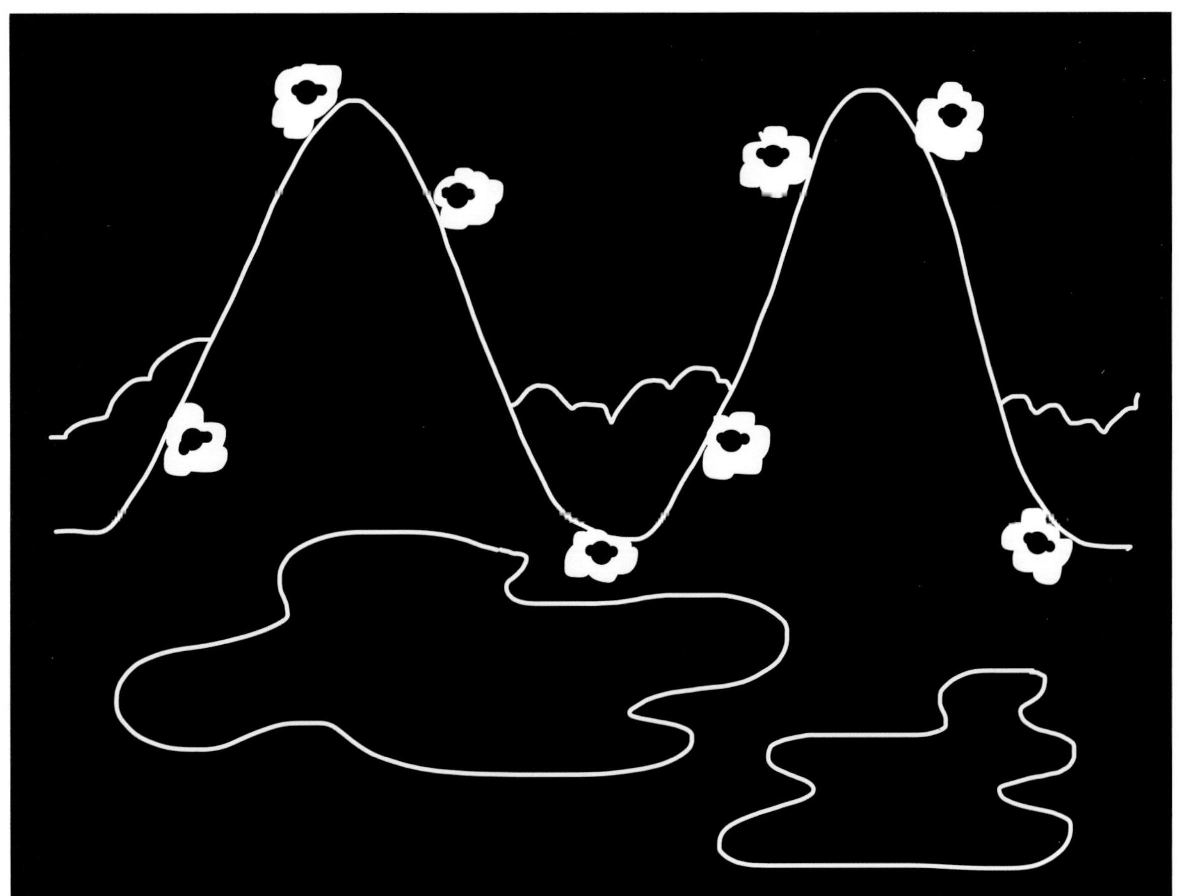

Turn this image upside down and the valleys become snow-topped peaks, while the flatland ponds turn into fluffy clouds. But the sheep still graze on happily.

Two for the Price of One

This chirpy owl conceals a secret. Can you work out what it is?

Just turn the page 90 degrees clockwise and the owl does something no other animal can do.

It changes into a fish.

In the illustration below we have plenty of wine glasses sitting on shelves, but no wine. Or is that true? Perhaps those are green wine bottles sitting on the shelves? Either way, the gaps between the glasses or bottles give a strong impression of the other. If only real life was so convenient!

Face- off

Do you see a vase?

...or two faces?

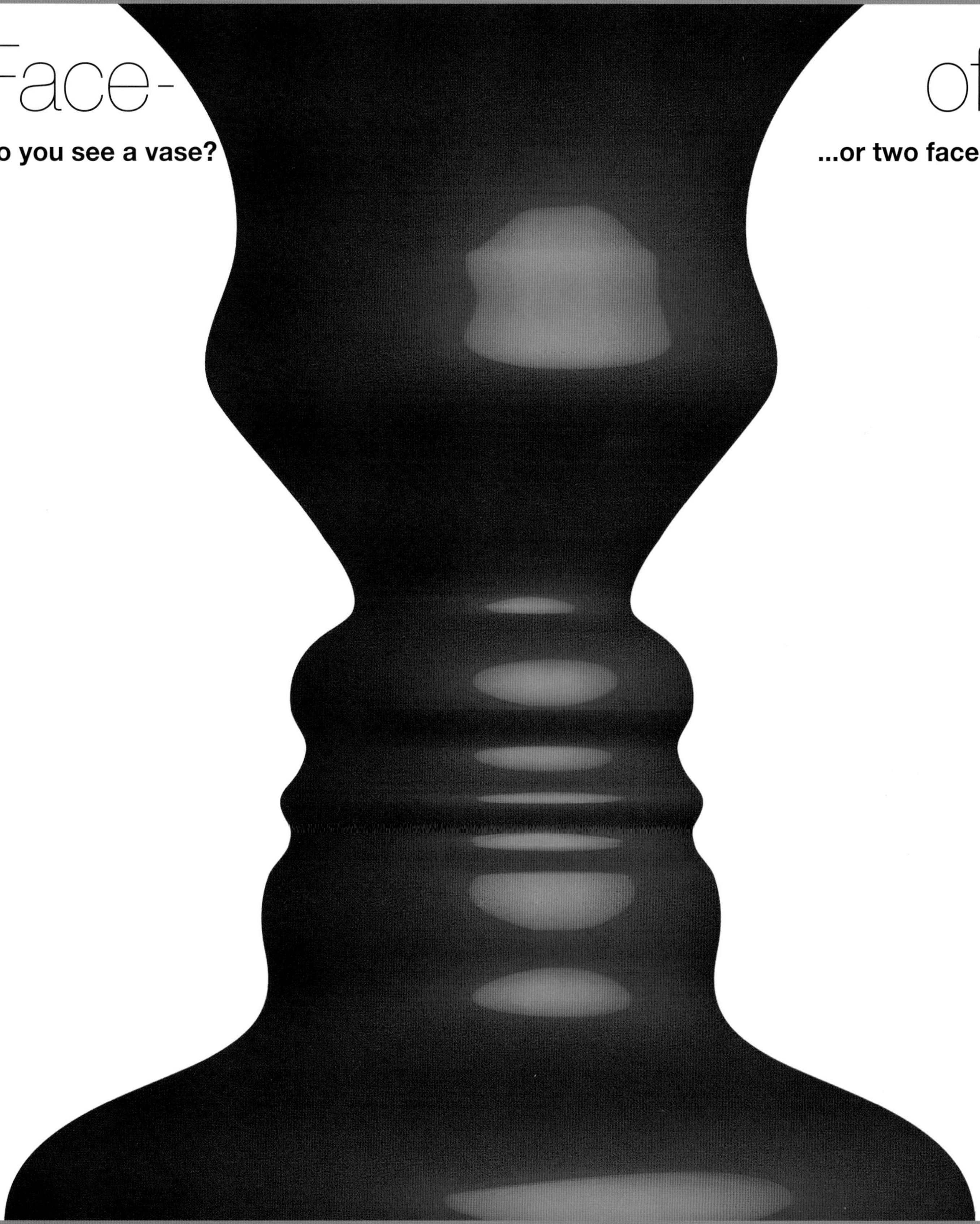

The Eyes Have It

Hold the book at arm's length and move it around. Do the eyes follow you?

No matter how you position the book, the eyes in the photograph below follow you around. This is because when eyes look straight forward we interpret them as looking directly at us, even when rationally we know that this character isn't really looking at anything—our automatic processing wins out.

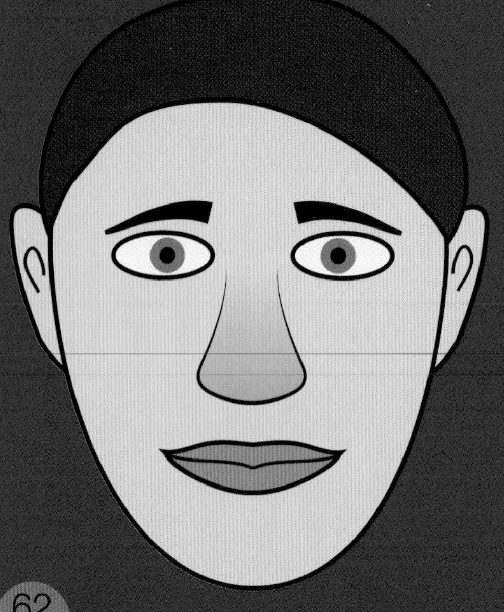

Interestingly, so strong is your visual processing that even if the eyes are moved into unnatural cross-eyed positions, as in the picture to the left, or away from the center, as on the right, you still see the faces as looking forward. So long as the eyes are symmetrical around the nose, our visual system can't conceive of any other explanation.

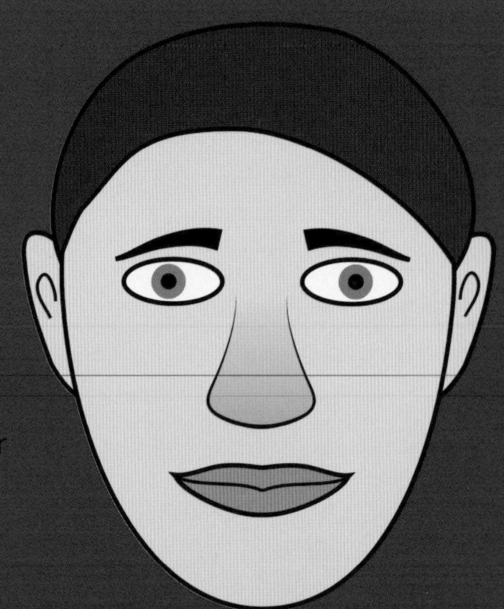

A Question of Focus

Is this face angry or calm?

Hold the book close and you see a calm face. Put the book down, step back and the face becomes angry.

How does this work? There are two faces, one overlaid on the other but heavily blurred. When you increase your distance from the image the blurred, upper image becomes more prominent. The lower, in-focus image is now partially obscured.

Facing Facts

They're watching you everywhere you go. How many faces do you see?

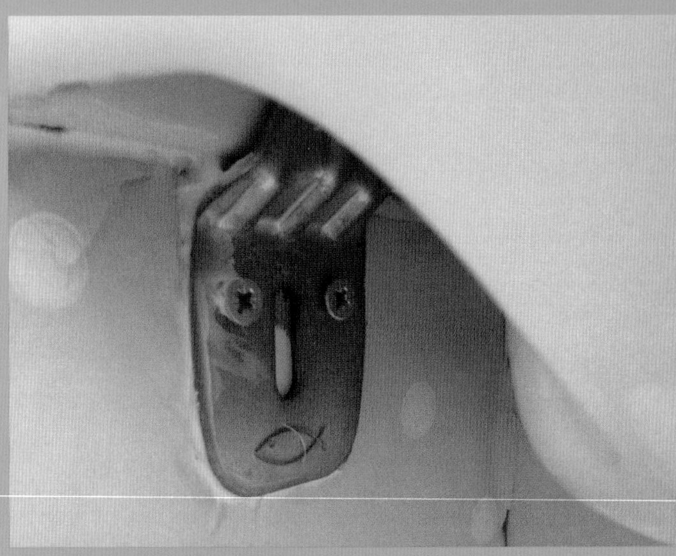

A cheeky satellite dish and a surprised sink bracket both seem to conceal faces. A wine bottle opener and the zip on a pocket also seem to be on the verge of coming to life.

Once you start looking for faces, you'll start seeing them everywhere!

Eye in the Sky

Is that roof really watching me?

The brain is so amazingly fantastic at spotting faces that it is almost impossible not to see the black soot marks on this roof as a giant eye, staring right back at you.

Even though there are no other facial elements present, the effect is still very strong.

A Shadowy Face

Shadow or nose?

Ever since humankind first looked up at the sky and saw the man lurking in the moon, or hunters dancing among the stars, our ability to spot faces in even the most unlikely places has been amply demonstrated.

Even in situations where we know there can't possibly be a human face, we still see them as clearly as if they were real.

And not just that, but we attach character and make associated deductions just as we would do if they really were people.

Your face tells the world a lot about you. Some of it you can control and some of it you can't. But if you looked like the house to the left, you'd probably be feeling quite cheeky.

Once a day, when the sun is in the right position, this hidden face is revealed to the world.

A Natural Visage

Rock faces are aptly named.

The name says it all: "rock face".

Can you find faces lurking in these remarkable features from the equally aptly named Remarkable Rocks?

They're found on Kangaroo Island, Australia.

Facial Features

Do you spot anything unusual about the upside-down version of this picture?

The image of a man is repeated here. On the left the photograph is in its usual orientation, and to the right it is flipped upside down. Although you might not be able to say for sure whether the pictures were identical, you would probably agree that both appear to be normal photographs of a human face. But are they?

Superficially, both images seem to be correct. We have no trouble spotting either of them as a normal, human face. Human beings rarely hang upside down from the ceiling, so we're not used to looking at them the wrong way up. We are, however, excellent at identifying typical facial features, as the photographs on the preceding pages have helped illustrate.

Try turning the book around to view the upside-down picture right way up. The differences should become clear immediately, and may well be surprising—clearly this is not a regular human face after all! Both eyes and the mouth have been reversed, and seen right side up the changes are very obvious. And yet turn the book back to normal orientation and the face will once again seem perfectly reasonable.

Visual Assumptions

Which one of these faces is more masculine?

Even though both images are of the same original photograph, the brightness cues on faces are used by the brain to make immediate snap decisions about issues such as gender. Differing contrast between facial elements is just one of the cues that you automatically use, whether you want to or not. Altering this contrast, as here, can influence your assignment of likely gender!

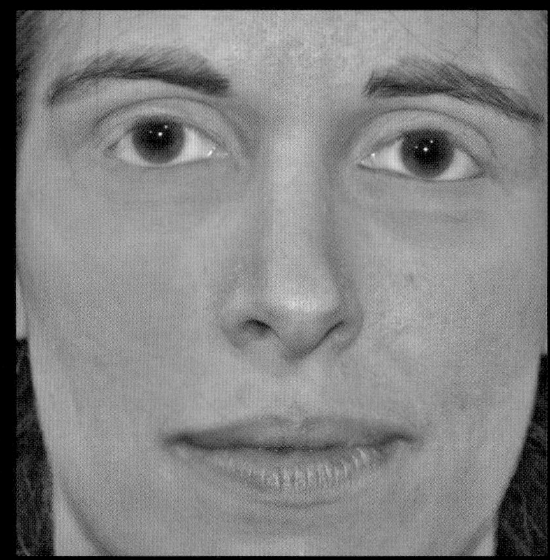

Is the receptionist really wearing shorts?

The brain is very good at making inferences, which is lucky for us because otherwise we'd have to do a lot of work just to make sense of everyday life. It particularly likes to associate objects which lie in a straight line.

In this picture, at first glance we may be surprised that the man wearing a suit top is wearing shorts behind the desk, but in truth there is a mirror beneath the desk which is reflecting the customer's legs.

Who's Counting?

How many birds are there?

Look at the top of the illustration to the left and you see four beautiful flamingos standing proud. But look instead at the bottom of the picture and you find there are now seven of them.

Where did the three extra birds come from?

Now look at the top of the picture below. There are four ostriches, happily enjoying their place in this book. But look instead at the bottom of the picture and there's an imposter! An extra bird has crept up and joined the group. Each half of the picture makes perfect sense on its own, so at a glance it's easy not to notice that the two halves don't quite fit together.

Who's That?

Who is the subject of this mosaic?

If you hold the page to the left fairly near to you, then you'll see a very large number of photos of California. Superimposed on top you might also make out the ghostly image of a face.

But put the book down and step as far back as you can and take another look. A well-known face becomes remarkably clear.

Shades of Gray

Are these solid gray rectangles a uniform color from top to bottom?

Look at the two rectangles marked with arrows. These vertical gray bars are the same color throughout, yet appear to fade from darker to lighter gray. Surrounding tints and shades have a great influence on our perception of color.

In the picture below, start at the right-hand red arrow and follow around the rectangle edge until you reach the other red arrow. Are the sections which the arrows point at different shades? Use decoder D to check.

D

D

Glowing Highlights

Is it possible to be whiter than white?

In the illustration to the right it seems as if the left-hand white edge of each shaded square is glowing slightly brighter than the underlying paper color. Yet as decoder B will prove, there is only one shade of white here.

The brain is interpreting the shading as if it represented light falling on a column or surface, and concludes that this part must be really very bright to shine like this.

The effect can be made even stronger if we use multiple cues to convince the brain that there must be a huge amount of light hitting a surface. In the top-left picture below, the white color inside each of the two crosses appears to glow considerably brighter than the paper. Use decoder B to check that this is just an illusion.

An opposite effect does not apply with a black background, as shown in the top-right picture below. In fact, the presence of the gray areas around the centers of the crosses actually makes the black look slightly paler, not darker.

Adding solid borders around the shapes, essentially telling the brain precisely where the edge actually is, greatly reduces the glow effect, as the illustrations below reveal.

Coloring *In*

Are there two shades of gray disk?

If we draw light or dark lines over a color, as in the illustration at the bottom left of this page, it's perhaps not especially surprising that this influences our perception of the underlying color. In this case the central square looks a slightly brighter blue than the background. The secret of this trick is revealed if you stand far enough back—the colors appear to mix into two very different shades of blue.

But the illusion to the right is quite different. There appear to be two different shades of gray disk, alternating back and forth by row. Decoder B will, however, reveal that they are all in fact exactly the same color and the surrounding colors are influencing your perception.

B

Influential Colors

Do you see three shades each of blue, yellow, green and red?

Looking at the picture below, it appears that each group of colors consists of light, mid and dark shades.

Follow each colored bar down to the bottom of the page, however, and it soon becomes clear that in fact there is only one shade of each color. As this demonstrates, it's the interleaved black and white bars that trigger this illusion.

Crossed Colors

Are the green columns on this page identical colors?

These green bars look very different shades, but decoder A will confirm they are identical shades.

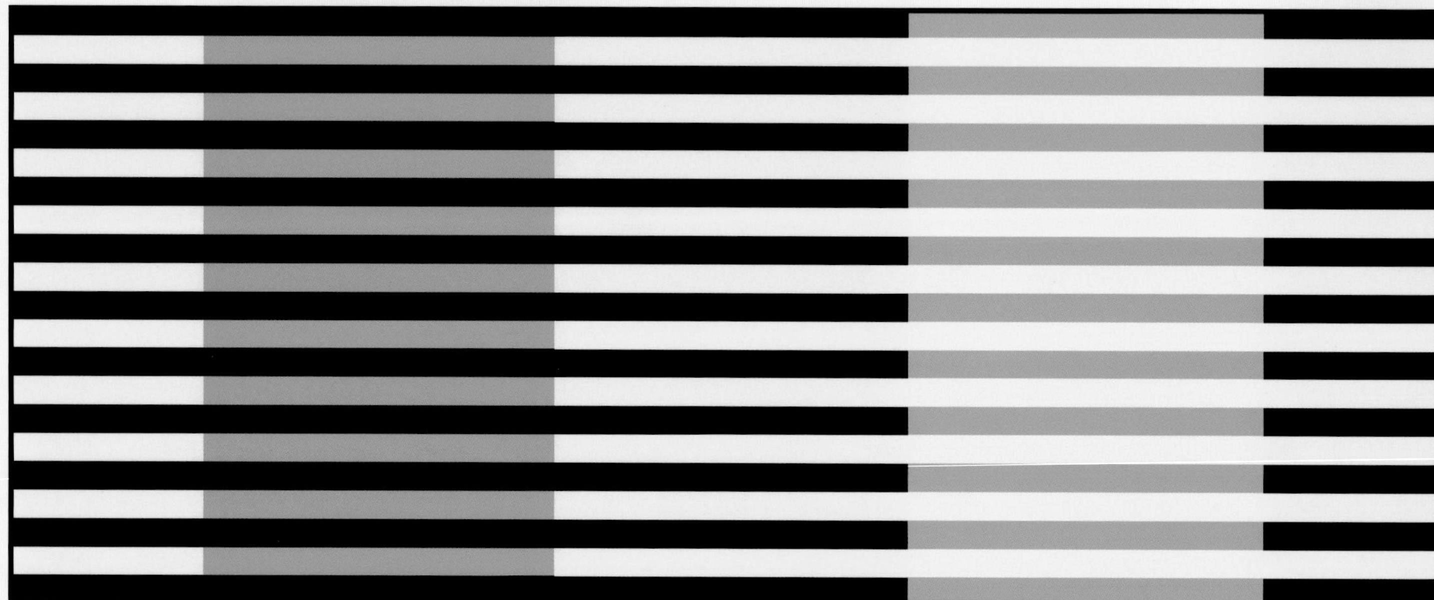

It's possible to extend this illusion further by interleaving more than two colors. Consider the picture below, where there seem to be three different pastel shades of vertical bar. In fact, each of the three bars is made of the same pure white. The perceived colors are formed via different mixes of the three crossing colors. You may need to hold the page at arm's length to see this illusion clearly.

Spreading **Color**

Does the paper change color on this page, or is it universally white?

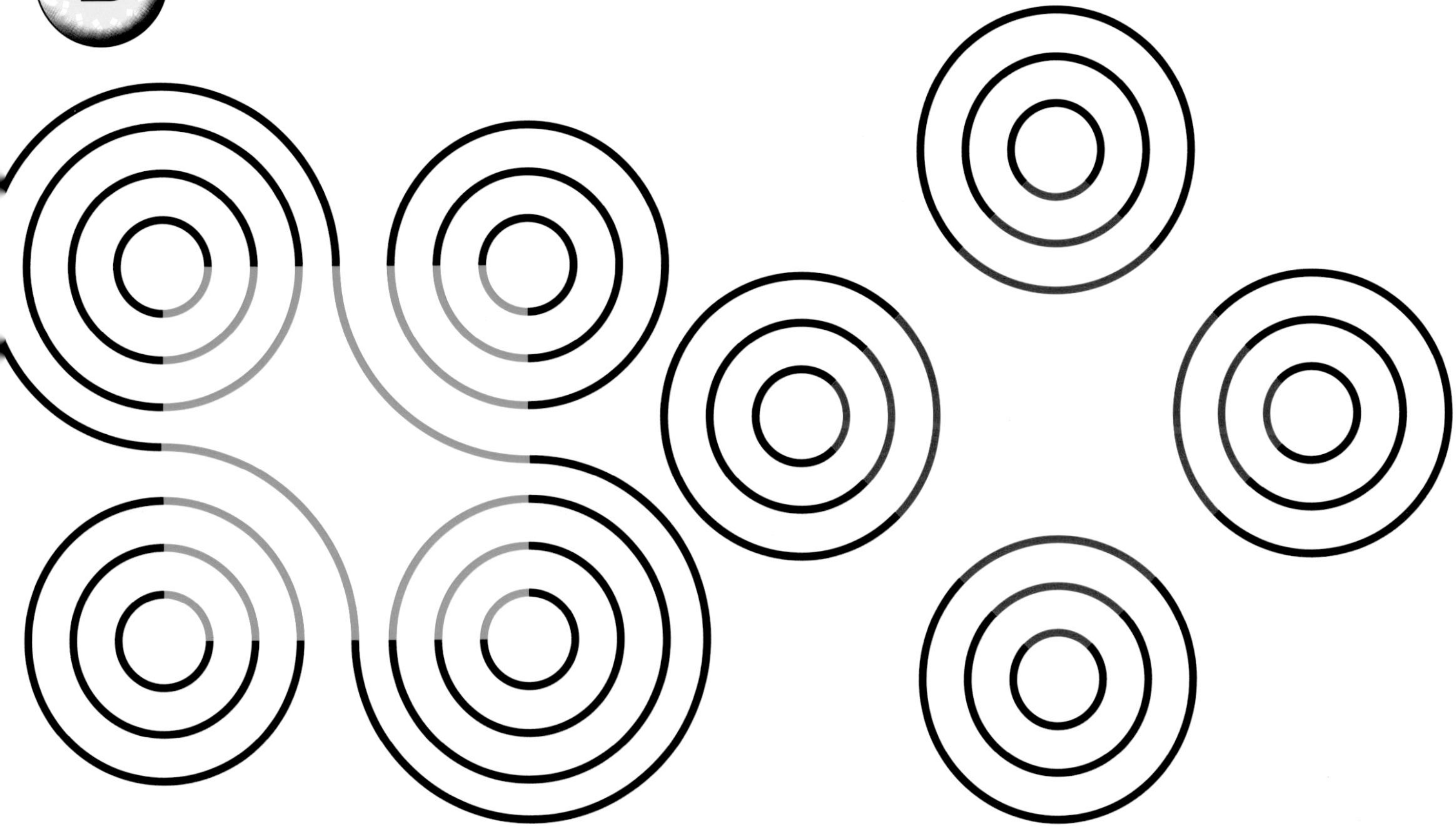

The colored segments on these circles and curves suggest that you can see squares, even though the squares themselves aren't actually drawn in. These implied squares in turn suggest that the paper the imagined squares cover is itself colored, so the chances are that you can see a faint green and a faint red color in the interior area of each square. But use decoder B to examine the paper and they will vanish.

Color can also leak into an area. Does this bow-tie shape below appear to be colored a faint blue?

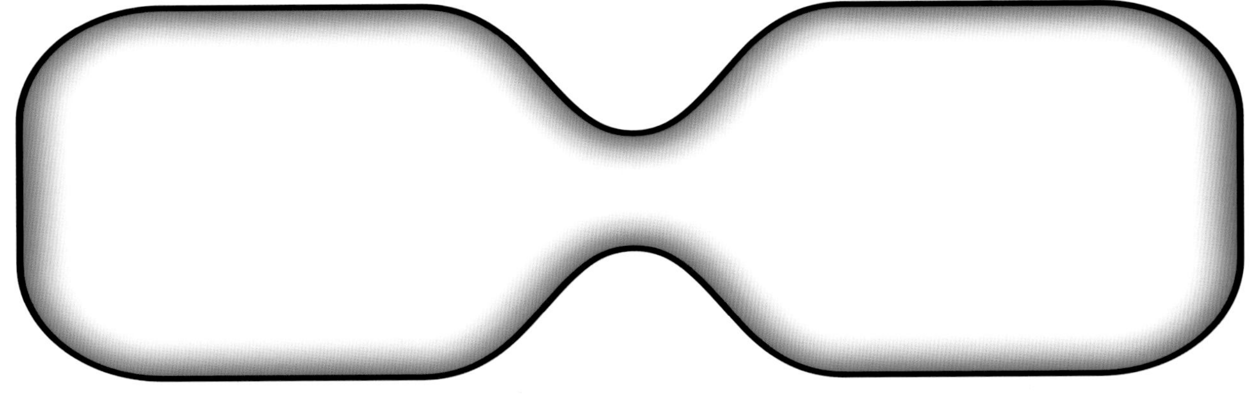

Color Gradations

B

Do you see four crossed boxes on this page?

There seem to be four vividly colored crosses on this page, and yet the surprising fact is that these crosses are entirely a figment of your imagination. The diagonals are no different in color to any other part of their surrounding area. You may be able to see this by using decoder B.

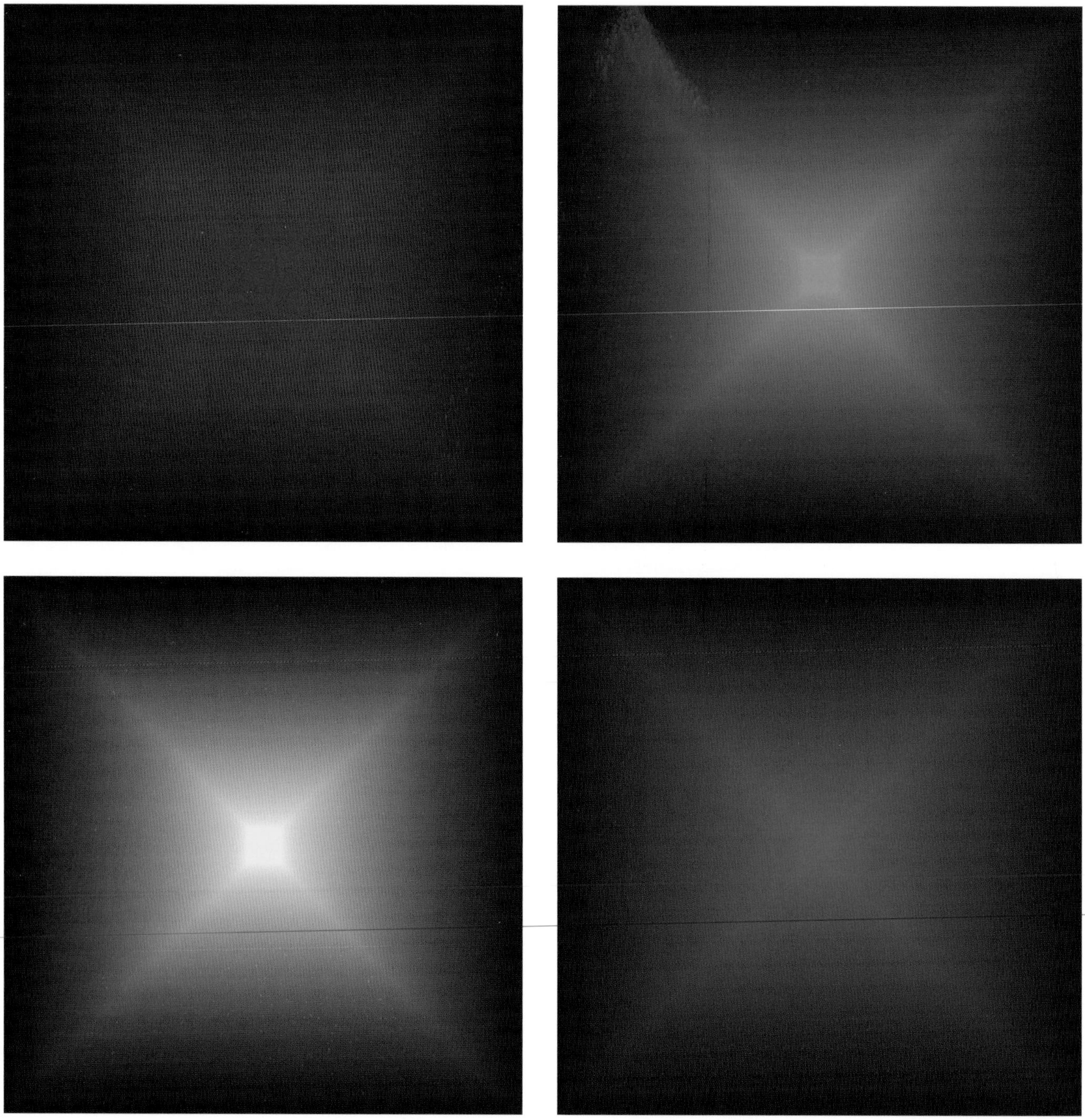

Color **Correction**

What color is the tile in the center of each of these four images?

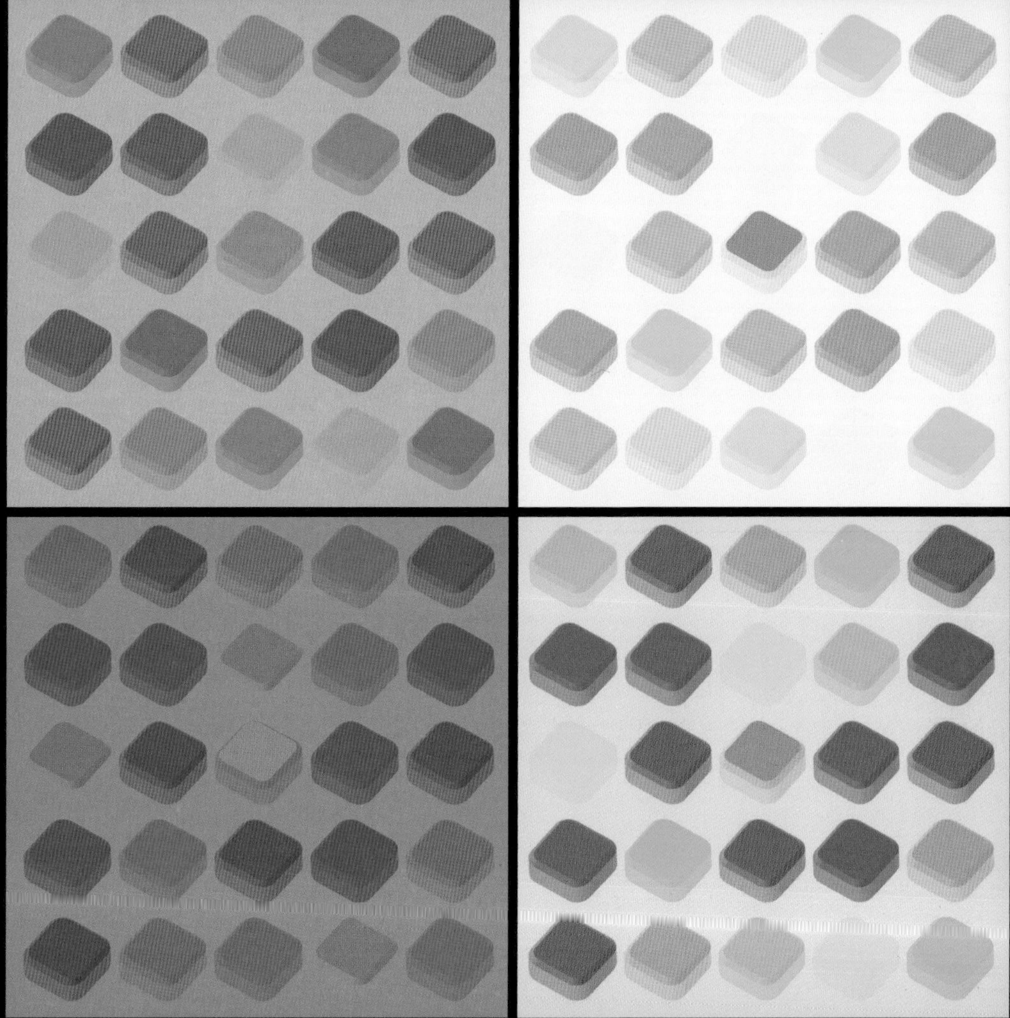

B

In the top left, the center tile appears to be green, while in the top right it's a deep blue and in the bottom left it's a pale yellow. The tile in the bottom right is a pale purple.

Meanwhile, the tile to the right of this text appears to be a colorless gray shade. Right?

Check these center tiles with decoder B, which will help reveal the remarkable truth that these are in fact all exactly the same color. All five tiles are precisely the same gray as shown on the single tile to the right. Your brain is color-correcting based on the surrounding hues. As you can see, this effect is incredibly powerful and, no matter how hard you try, quite impossible to disable.

Reading **Skills**

Perform the sum in the first triangle, then read the second one aloud.

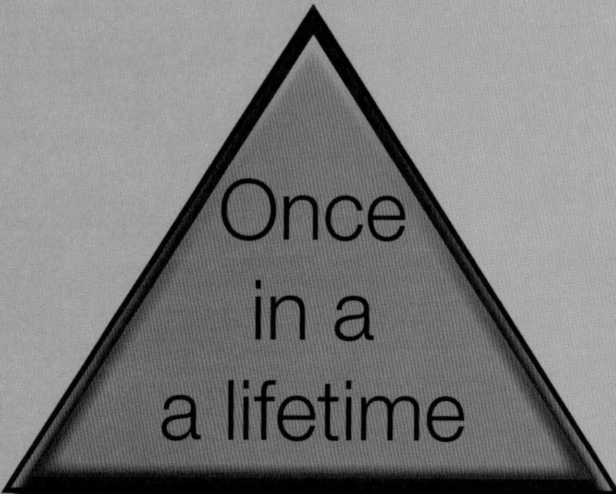

Did you notice what was wrong with each of these instructions? If you didn't, then read them again. Your brain tidied up the errors to the point where you were completely unaware they were there.

Now try reading the text below and count the number of letter "f"s in the mildly strange story.

Finally found in Finland was the result of centuries of scientific research into fog and foreign imports of smog and stuff.

How many "f"s did you count? Was it the total given on page 96?

Parsing Text

Can you read the text on this page? Can you solve the sum in your head?

Almost evrey wrod hsa ahd smoe of ist ltrtees rerrngaaed.

Tsi ucmh darhre ot eard ehwn oattyll xemid pu!

You probably found that with a bit of thought you could read most of the first sentence, "Almost every word has had some of its letters rearranged." But chances are that you couldn't make head or tail of the second one. This is because we use the first and, to a lesser extent, last letters of a word as a key part of identifying it. Change the first letter and we find it considerably harder to work out what the word was meant to be.

The second sentence, in case you were wondering, reads "It's much harder to read when totally mixed up!".

Now take a look at the sum on the right. Work out the answer in your head before reading any further.

Have you tried the sum? Did you get a total that was an exact multiple of one thousand? If you did, then you got it wrong, although you're in good company since it's a common mistake. Most people confuse magnitudes when adding up numbers such as these. Your brain is trying to be helpful by assuming the numbers are similar, even when they aren't. The actual solution is given on page 96.

$$
\begin{array}{r}
1000 \\
30 \\
1000 \\
10 \\
20 \\
1020 \\
1000 \\
+\quad 20 \\
\hline
????
\end{array}
$$

Reading in the **Dark**

Can you read all four pieces of text in the white boxes?

Each of the boxes has disguised the text in different ways, and yet you can still read the words. The first shows only the gaps between the letters, reading "Paris." The second has only shadows cast behind its letters and reads "Mexico." The final case overlays two words, which can still be read with suitable concentration. It reads "New York" on the paler layer and "Florida" on the darker layer.

Text *Art*

What do you see?

At first glance this page seems to be full of random letters and symbols, but hold the page further away or partially close your eyes and you'll see the clear image of a parrot. Pieces of eight!

```
;;;;;;;;;;;;;;;;;;;;;;;;;;;;;;;;;;;;;;;;;;;;;;;;;;;;;;;;;;;;;;;;;;;;;;;;;;;;;;;;;;;;;;;;;;;;;;;;;;;;
;.:::::::::::::::::::::::::::::::::::::::::::::::::::::::::::::::::::::::::::::::,,,:::::::::::
;;;;;;;;;;;;;;;;;;;;;;;;;;;;;;;;;;;;;;;;;;;;;;;;;;;;;;;;;;;;;;;;;;;;;;;;;;;;;;;;;;;;;;;;;;;;;;;:
;;;;;;;;;;;;;;;;rrrrrrrrrrrrrr;;;;;;;;;;;;;;;;;;;;;;;;;;;;;;;;;;;;;;;;;;;;;;;;;;;;;;;;;;;;;;;;;;:
;;;;;;;;;;;;;;;;rrr;:,,..,:;;;;;r;;;;;;;;;;;;;;;;;;;;;;;;;;;;;;;;;;;;;;;;;;;;;;;;;;;;;;;;;;;;;;;:
;;;;;;;;;;;;;;;rr:.              ,rrr;;r;;;;;;;;;;;;;;;;;;;;;;;;;;;;;;;;;;;;;;;;;;;;;;;;;;;;;;;;:
;;;;;;;;;;;;;;r;;,    .  ..     .,r;rr;;rrsr;;;;;;;;;;;;;;;;;;;;;;;;;;;;;;;;;;;;;;;;;;;;;;;;;;;;
;;;;;;;;;;;;;;Sr.  ., .;;rr;,,:;;;rr;;rrissss;::;;;;;;;;;;;;;;;;;;;;;;;;;;;;;;;;;;;;;;;;;;;;;;;;
;:;;;;;;;;;;;rM&i,,:::;r;rsrr;rsr:    .rrssSXSr;:;;;;;;;;;;;;;;;;;;;;;;;;;;;;;;;;;;;;;;;;;;;;;;;
;:;;;;;;;;;;;@@G9932XSri2Xh9SSi,  rAHi,rrsiS55Sr:::;;;;;;;;;;;;;;;;;;;;;;;;;;;;;;;;;;;;;;;;;;;;;
;:;;;;;;;;;;:,h#ri&@@2S293BM925;  H@@@@.,rrrsissi;,,::::::;;;;;;;;;;;;;;;;;;;;;;;;;;;;;;;;;;;;;:
;,;;::::::::,;.  2@#XiiS;riX3i;,;@@@@A .;rrsrrsiir:,,,:::::::::;;;;;;;;;;;;;;;;;;;;;;;;;;;;;;;;:
:,:::::::::,,. ,  :    :    ;ss;.,;Si .rrsssiiisi5i;.,,,,,::::::::;;;;;;;;;;;;;;;;;;;;;;;;;;;;;:
:,::::::::::::.:r.        .     ,:;,     ,rsSisriisiiSX:.,,,,,::::::::::;;;;;;;;;;;;;;;;;;;;;;;;:
:,:::::::::;;:5Sr.   :ri9.            ,rsiiisssSiiiXi;..,,,,,,:::::::::::::;;;;;;;;;;;;;;;;;;;;;:
:,:::::::::ir59AA25rG@@@2:.          ..:riisiiiSssiiS52:..,,,,,:::::::::::::::;;;;;;;;;;;;;;;;;:
:,::::::::;@@&A#@@@#@Asrr;,,.....  ..,;ssiiiiisrris2X32r,.,,,,::::::::::::::::::::;;;;;;;;;;;;;:
:,:::::::,s@B3A@@HHAGriSr:,,,,.,,,,:::S2Siissiirssi;iSsir:.,,,::::::::::::::::::::::::;;;;;;;;:
:,;;::::::,s@MA#MG&X2Si5i;,:::;::::;;rrrS5iiiirSiisss:issis22;:,,,,::::::::::::::::::::::::;;;;:
:,;;::::::,:@@B#MAAh2iir:;:;;;rr;;;rrisssssissrssisSr;ss;sisS55Ss;:,,,:::::::::::::::::::::::;;:
;,;;;;;;;:,.A@Xi;@#MBA&3S5;;;;;rrr;;rrrrrsrrrsrssisisrrr;;iiiii2XXSr;:,::::::::::::::::::::::::;
:,;;;;;;;;:.:@M, s@##MAA9&Xsrr;;rrrr;;rrrrrrrissirsh9X;rrrssrrssi522X92r:,,::::::::::::::::::::;
;,;;;;;;;;:, s@,  ##AG2isiS5rs55issrssrrrrssiisii2HMB5,riSisissss55SSi23Xs;:::;;;;;;;;;;;;;;;;;;
:,;;:::;;:,. ., i@A&25522iiisisiSSiissSiiirsS9BHA#3 riiiiiiisiiiSS5SS522ir:::;;;;;;;;;;;;;;;;;;;
:,;:::::::,,;,..MMA3ir;sSssiii5SsiiisiSSiiiS9AGAB#@,:5siSss5iS22Si222X25232s;::;;;;;;;;;;;;;;;;;
;,;;::;;;;;;::::, 2@AAXir;rsssiisiSSiiiiiSS25S59&AB#@Hiisiisriiii52255S599XSSX2ir;;;;;;;;;;;;;rr;
;:;;;;;;;;;;;;;;:.;@AHH3552X2isSSisiSiSiiSS5is2HHBM#@@@rrSiSSSsisriii2ii22392i2XXSsr;;rrr;;;;;;;;rrrrrrrr;
;:rrrr;;;;;;;;;;;;:.AMHB&XssiS5isSS55SSSS5SS5Si2HAA&AM@@&.s25SsssiirissS252522XX2S2X3Xs;rrrrrrrrrrrrrrrsssr
r;rrrrrrrrrrrrrr;;.i#3hBAG3X2X9932SSi5222SSssis3AGGAB#@@sriirsisS2S52sXG52iiS52XSii2hGSrrrrrrrrrrrrsssssir
srsssrrrrrrrrrrr;::AHhAAHAhSS55552255SSiii5SSii9hhAHM#@@:rrrsSiiS5iis95iSSiii2X52S2hGXirrsssssssssssiiiir
sriiiisssssssrrrrr;::B@h5ShAhXSiSS5iiiiiiS2SiS5s2hGAHBM@@h;;SrsSisissr;XX522X2533i5XX9A332Sssssssssssssiiis
is5SSiiiiiissssssrr;:;&BGGA3hX&hX5222SssiSiiiiisshAAAHM#@@2;s5iiissrrri9252XXXS22ss2XS2SiXGSrsssssssssssiiis
Si2555SSSiiisssssssrrr::s#@AX3GG3X2SSS5555SS5SiSisGAG&AH#@@@s;sssiSiss3hXSiii55SSSirs5i5XSi295rssrsssssssiiis
5SX2?255SSiiissssssssrrr:::5##XS55?5??2?5?XXX?5SiSSi2GG&AAB#@@&srrri5?XX9X?SSiSiiS5??5iiiiX3S53&?siirrrsssssir
5i2255SSSiiisssssrrrrrrr;;,s@HX5ii55552X25555SS55ii&&GAHBM#@@XisrriS5222SS2i55i2222X2Si553XiXh92isr;;rrrrrrr
Ss5SSiiissrrrrrrrrrrrr;;;;;:,9@M&925S23X252XX225iiSSXG9AHBB##@@X5rrSi555222SSX5i3X2S23XiSSS2S53is55Sr;;;;;rr;
isSiiissssrrrrrrrrrrrr;;;;;:iM#H322XX2SSS225S5222SiiAGAAAHM#@@B25rS2S5SS5222SiX925iS392S2255229253X2s;:;;;r;
isSSiiisssrrrrrrrrrrrrrr;;;:r#@@@#B&AhX223252h922SSs2A&&&ABM#@@G3ssXsS2iiS2SiXhXX5ii2X2552XS52X323AAhXs:;;r;
isSiiiiisssrrrrrrrrrrrrrrr;,s@@@HMB&h2X&933X25552isiGA&AABMM#@@X5rXiS2SiS2X29322Ss5222SS22X522XX259XhAi:;r;
isSiiissssssrrrrrrrrrrrrrr;;,A@@M##BAG92S232i52XXS555AAAHHBM#@@@Xr2iS2Xii22X3XX2iiS22Si52X9X225X3i2XX&B5;;;
isSiiiisssssrrrrrrrrrrrrrr;;,;@@@BHBMHG223X232X325SSs3HAAAHBM#@@#ss5iX3XiS552SSSSS5S5iS222XX2iX335s52XGHs;;
irSiiiiisssssrrrrrrrrrrrrr;;,9@@@#MAB#Ah3SS2255S5222S&AAAHBM##@@&sSs29hSSX2XSi225XXissS55XX2i3hX2Ssi529XS;
iriiissssssssrrsrrrrrrrrrrr;::@@@@#HA#MHG3XSi2S529X252AHHHBBM##@@2sis39Xi9GA3s2X52Xiiisii225S9h32X5rs52Xhs
iriiiisssssssrrrsrrrrrrrrrrr;,r@@@@#AAHA9XG93X52322222&HAHHBBBM@@@5rsi3&iXGA9iX922X52X2SiSSS23h922h2Si52Ai
iriiiisssssssssssssrrrrrrrrrr;:.5@@@@MAHHBBGXX5i33X25553AAAAHBBM#@@@Xrrsh2SGAAS3G92553333X555529X253GXS2i9i
iriisssssssssssssssrrrrrrrrrr;:.&@@@@#AABBHhS53325ii532GHAAHBMMMM@@@&rri3SX&A529h32S3hhXX5XX5X33X2XXXiS2is
iriissssssssssssssssssrrrrrrrrr;:,B@@@@@MAAHH&G9X2X3XXX22HBHHHBBBB#@@@#Srrsi3A25X93X2Xhh3X2Xh922XX2XX25i22s
iriiisiiissssssssssssssrrrrrrrrr;,,M@@@@@#BHMMAX553Xi5XX2GBAAAAHHB##@@@@#AS;shXiXh9X929hh3XX9h2SXX2293XSS3S
iriisiiiissssssssssssssrrrrrsrrr;,,A@@@@@@#HBBAAA95XG922XGAAAAAHBMM#@@@@@@h2r2i239XhX99hh923Gh5X9X2XGGXS5S
iriiiiiiiiiiiissssssssssssssssrrr;,.i@@@@@@@###@B9hG92S525G#BHHHHBMM###@@@@@Assi233GXXhGGG9XGA22hhX5XGG225
iriisiiiiiiiiiiiiissssssssssssssssrrr;:.,iB@@#@@#@###MMAh25255hAHBHBHBBHB###@@@@@2si29G929hGhGXhA929hG2X9G322
iriisiiiiiiiiiiiiiiissssssssssssssssrrrr;;,..,:. ..i@@#MB#B92X555iXG9&AABBBBMM#@@@@@hi5539SX999&39AA2XhGhXX9G22
iriiiiiiiiiiiiiiiiiiiisssssssssssssrrrrrr;;:,.,,,. ;#@@MM###M&X5222X99XAHAAAHM##@@@@A2X29XS3hhA&XAHGX9GGhX2h32
iriiiiiiiiiiiiiiiiiiiiissssssssssssssssrrrrr;;;;;;;:.,A@@@#MM##A9hX5Xh32i2AHHMMM##@@@@HX3X9259GAA9&AA33&&AA2XA2
irsrrrssssssssssssssssrrrrrrrrrrrrrrrrrr;;;;;;;;;;;;;;;;;;:iH@@#MMMBBBHHAG333X3&AHHBMM####@B9X225239hXXhGhX9hhGhXXX
```

Seeing with Two Eyes

Can you make a double-ended finger float in front of your eyes?

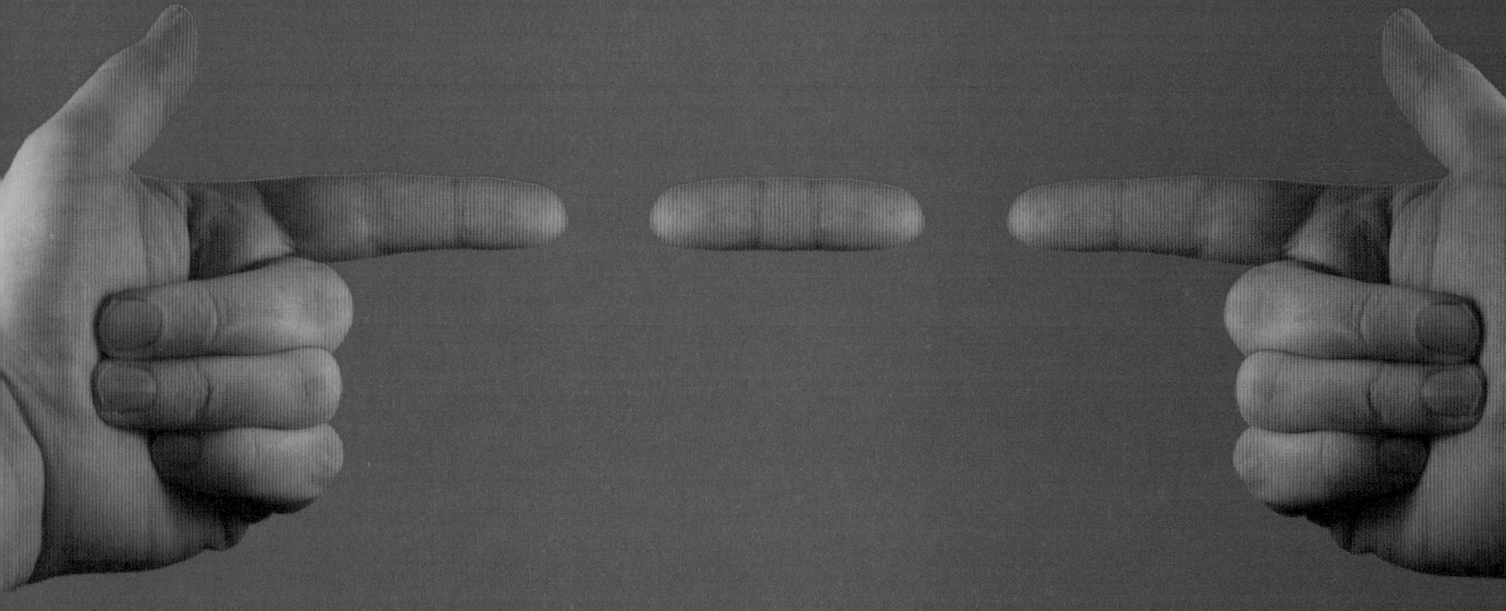

The separation between our eyes allows us to see the world in three dimensions. It's a critical ability for judging distance and for disambiguating a scene. However, when an item is extremely close to us then the distance between our two eyes can be enough to produce a confusing scene. For example, if you place a finger in front of each eye then you'll see an imaginary third finger, similar to the above.

By moving the page very close to your face, can you reunite the two halves of the shape below?

Stereoscopic Vision

Let yourself go cross-eyed on these images. What do you see?

Cross your eyes until your left eye seemingly stops on the right image and your right eye stops on the left image. At this point you should see a perfectly in-focus 3D picture just as if you were actually looking at the scene in person. If you have trouble seeing these, place a finger on the paper and slowly move it towards your nose while focusing on the finger. With practice the image should come into focus, and you should see it clearly.

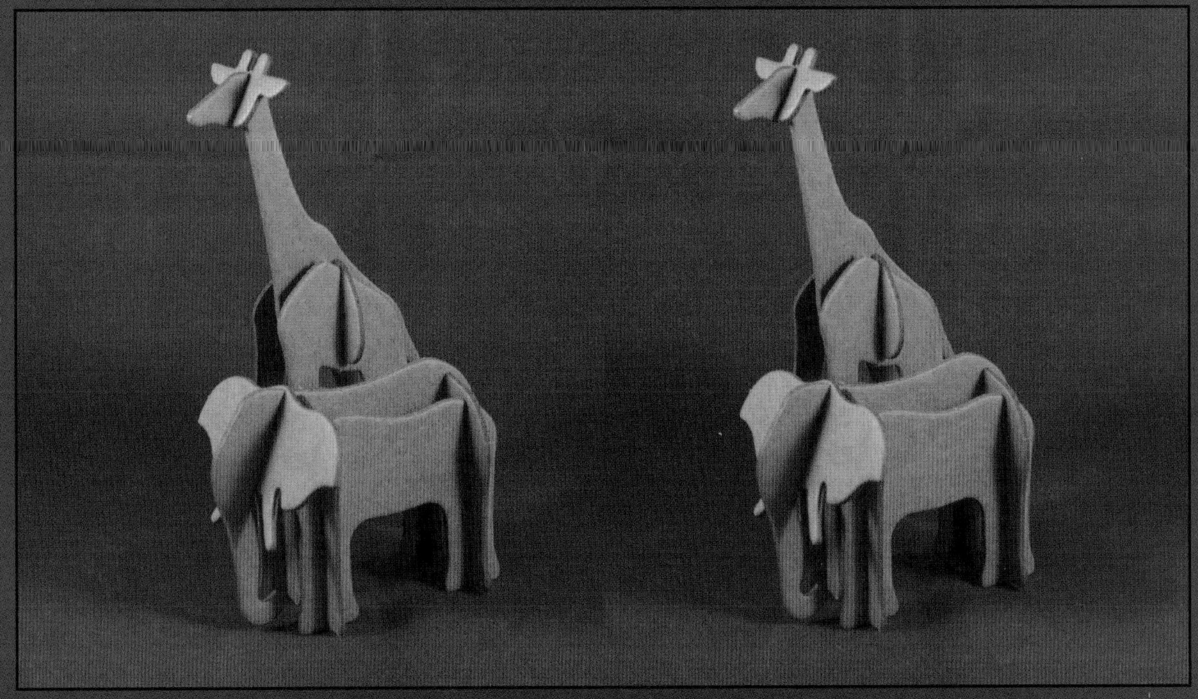

A *Staring* Contest

Stare at the bold text for 20 seconds, then look away at a white page or wall.

HELLO

The retina is the part of the eye that detects light, and it has certain properties which can be exploited by optical illusions. In particular, there is a persistence of vision effect which means that the retina continues to react to visual stimuli which it is no longer receiving. The duration of these effects is often related to the duration of the exposure of the original stimuli.

In this particular case, having first stared at the "HELLO," when you then look away at an empty white area you see a clear glowing "HELLO" projected in that space. Indeed, you see it clearly enough that you can actually still read it.

Now try staring at this set of concentric rectangles for 20 seconds, before looking at something white.

You should have been able to clearly see the inverse image, and what's particularly interesting is that not only do the solid black areas become glowing white borders, but the internal white areas also become darker and blacker.

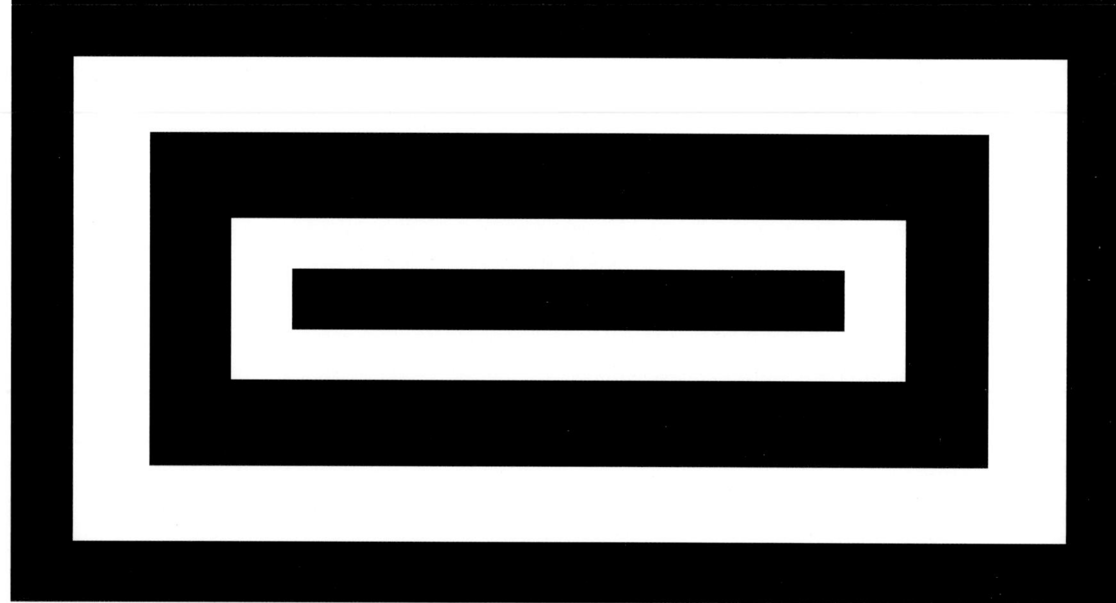

After Effects

Move your eyes slowly around each of these images.

Even if you don't consciously keep your eyes still first, you still see trailing dots. And, what's more, this happens whether on a white or a black background. This effect can feel surprisingly disorientating.

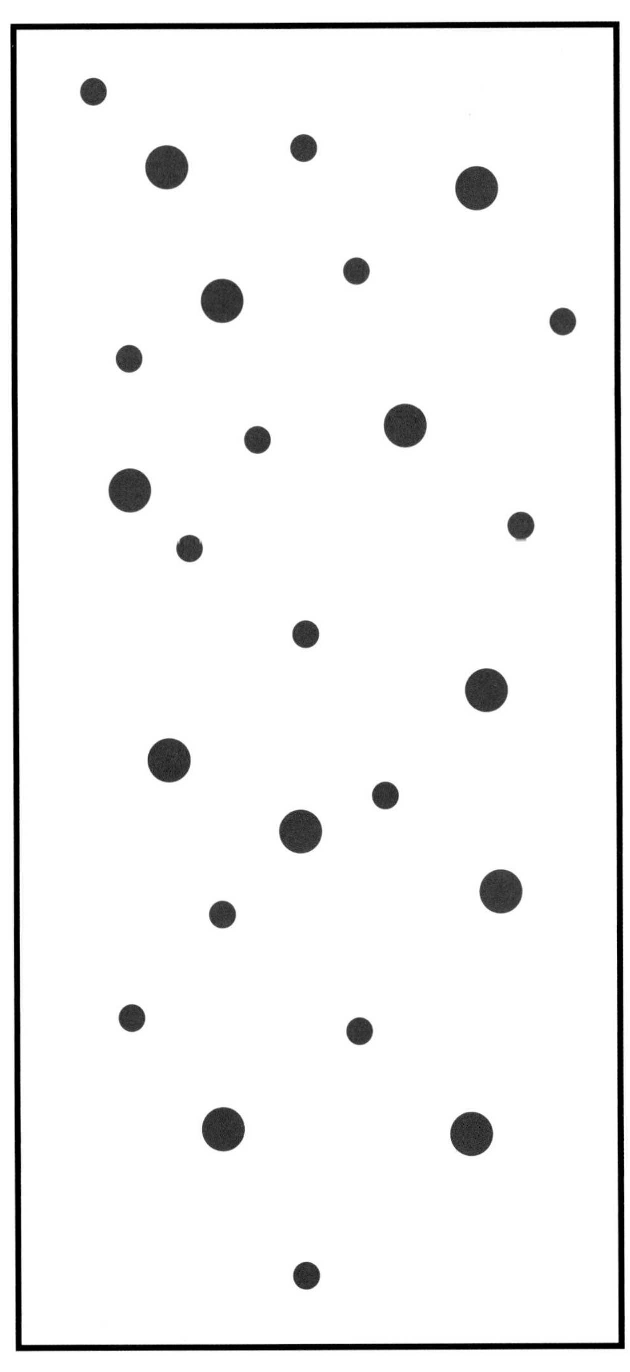

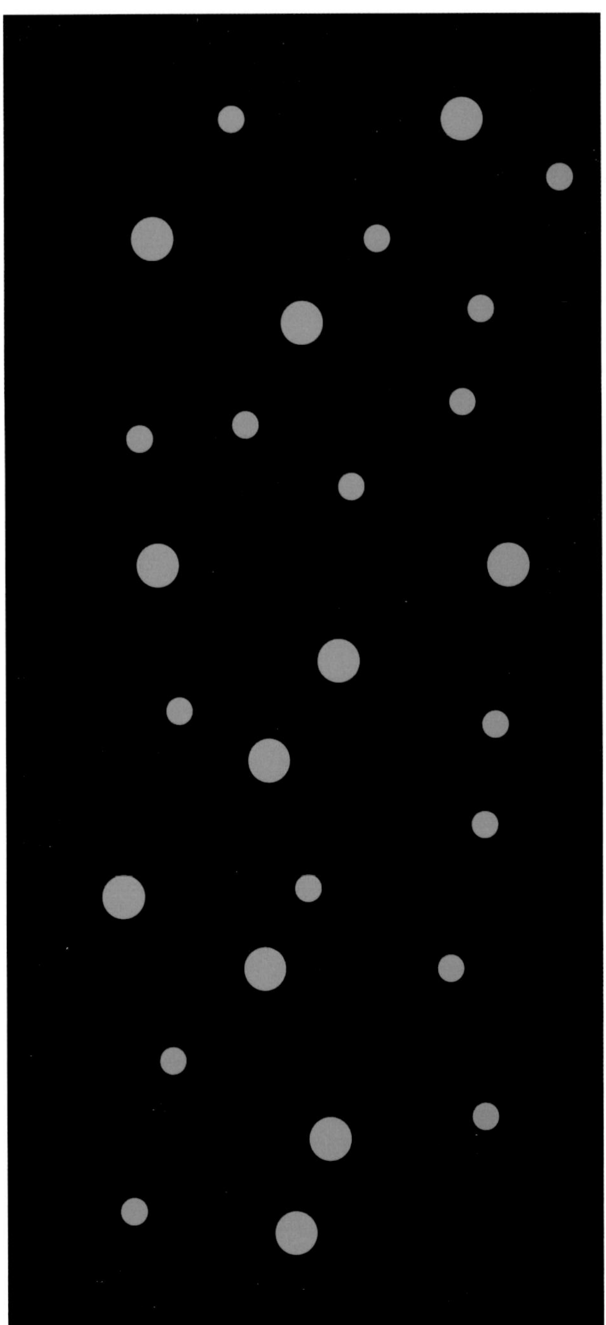

Complementary Colors

Stare at the picture below for 20 seconds, then look away at a white ceiling.

The effect you will see is pretty striking, with not just a glowing white lightbulb but also a vivid yellow filament inside. If you don't see the filament immediately, wait a second and it will appear—you should be able to see the details of the bulb clearly for at least a few seconds.

A Blind Spot

Close your right eye and look at the green cylinder. Slowly move the book closer.

Start with the book far enough away from you that you can clearly see all three cylinders with the right eye closed—so around two feet (half a meter) or more—and make sure that you continue to keep your eye shut and look directly only at the green disk. You should be able, however, to see the yellow and red disks in your peripheral vision.

As you move the book slowly closer, first the red disk vanishes, then it reappears, and then the yellow disk vanishes before eventually reappearing again.

This happens because there is a large blind area in each eye, where the optic nerve is attached. Ordinarily, you're not aware of it because the brain fills in information from the other eye and other parts of the scene, but when an isolated object isn't visible from either eye it will simply vanish, as shown here.

Here's another complementary color illusion, this time using inverse traffic lights. Rotate the book so that the purple circle is at the bottom, then stare at the rectangle for 20 seconds. Now look away at the furthest white ceiling or wall within eyesight. You will see glowing red, yellow and green disks. Again, give the illusion a moment to stabilize.

Getting **Tired**

Focus on the left-hand gray smudge until it vanishes.

If you look steadily at the gray area you might be surprised to find that it quickly starts to fade away until it is indistinguishable from the surrounding region. This only works so long as you keep your vision fixed on it, however.

This can even work when there are other distractions. Try staring at the right-hand smudge. You will probably find it takes longer to vanish, or you may see a gray disk surrounded by plain white paper.

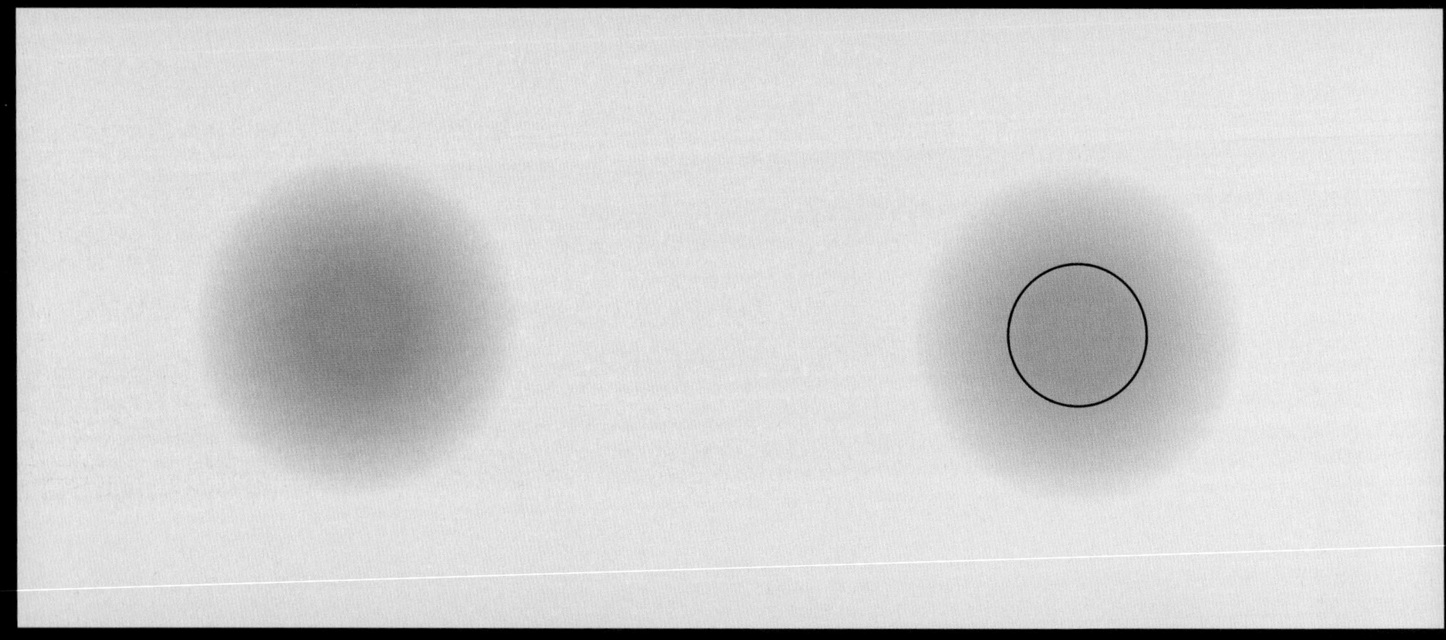

The eye can get tired of illusions too. Consider the picture on the right, where you should see a somewhat brighter area of paper in the center of the image caused by the implict yellow square.

Look at the illusion steadily for several seconds, however, and the bright area fades to the surrounding background area.

You need only look away for a brief moment for the illusion to be restored, however.

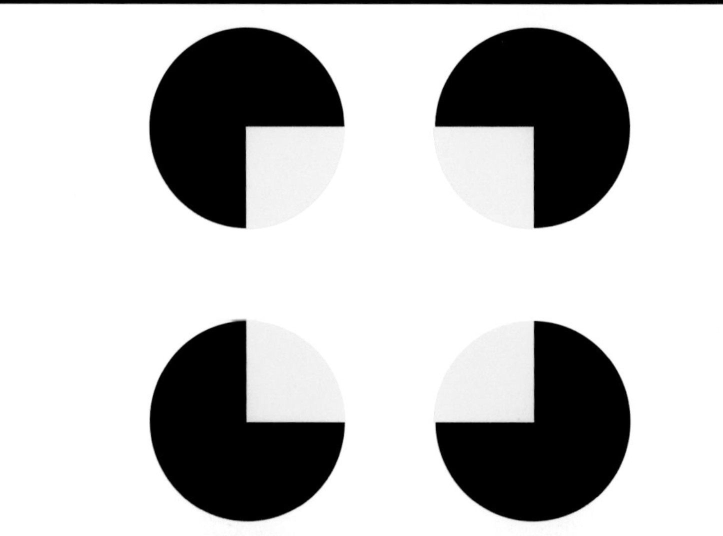

Lost in the **Clouds**

It's not just gray that can vanish. Stare at the orange glow below.

Focus on the center of the orange glow, right in the middle of the picture, and a remarkable illusion will unfold. First of all the surrounding magenta, yellow, cyan and green glowing areas will fade away to the background gray. Then, if you are patient, the orange area too will slowly fade away until, eventually, only a flat, gray square remains. You may need to hold the book quite close to you for this to work.

Filling in the **Blanks**

Do these gray disks appear to be floating in space?

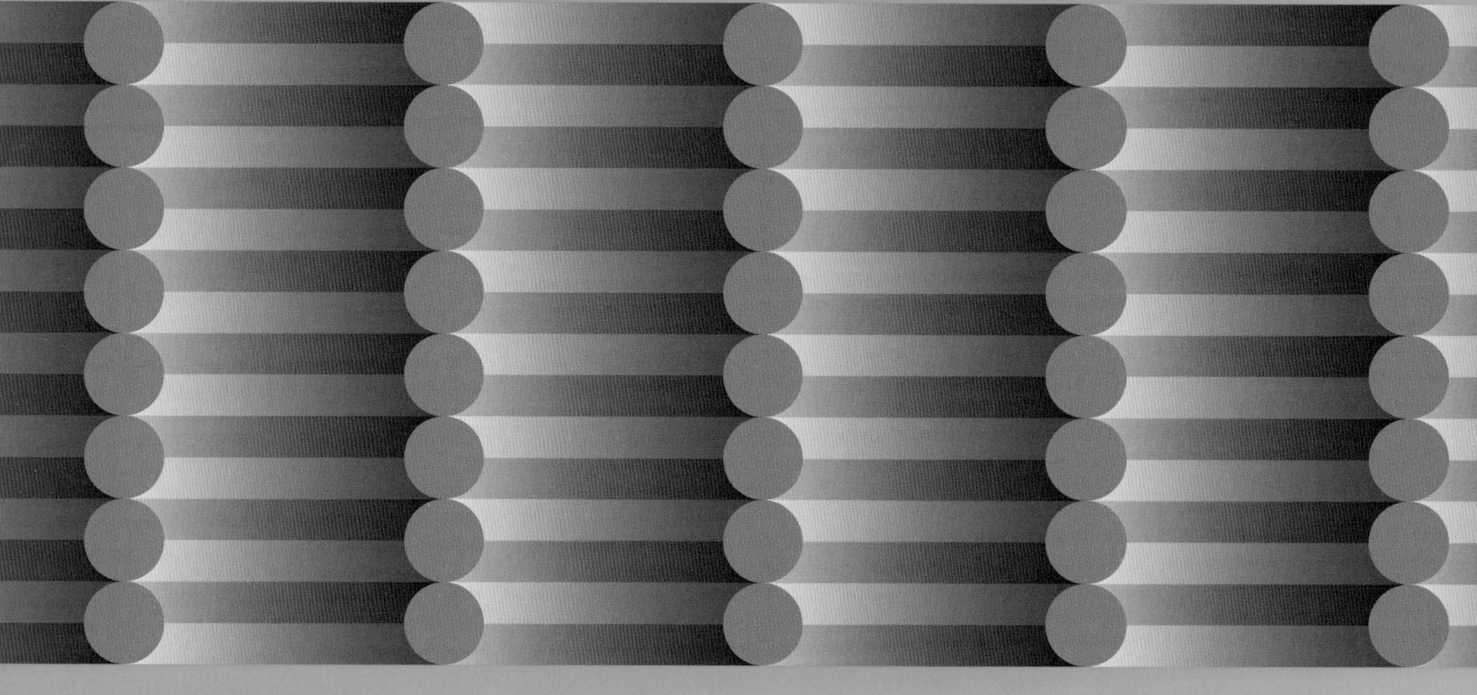

The impression of depth in the above picture is astonishing. Even when looking at the page with both eyes open, the interplay of shades gives the strong impression that the disks are floating on top, or that the colored bars are cut back behind the page.

Meanwhile, the grid to the right appears to be full of red circles, and yet they are really just crosses.

B

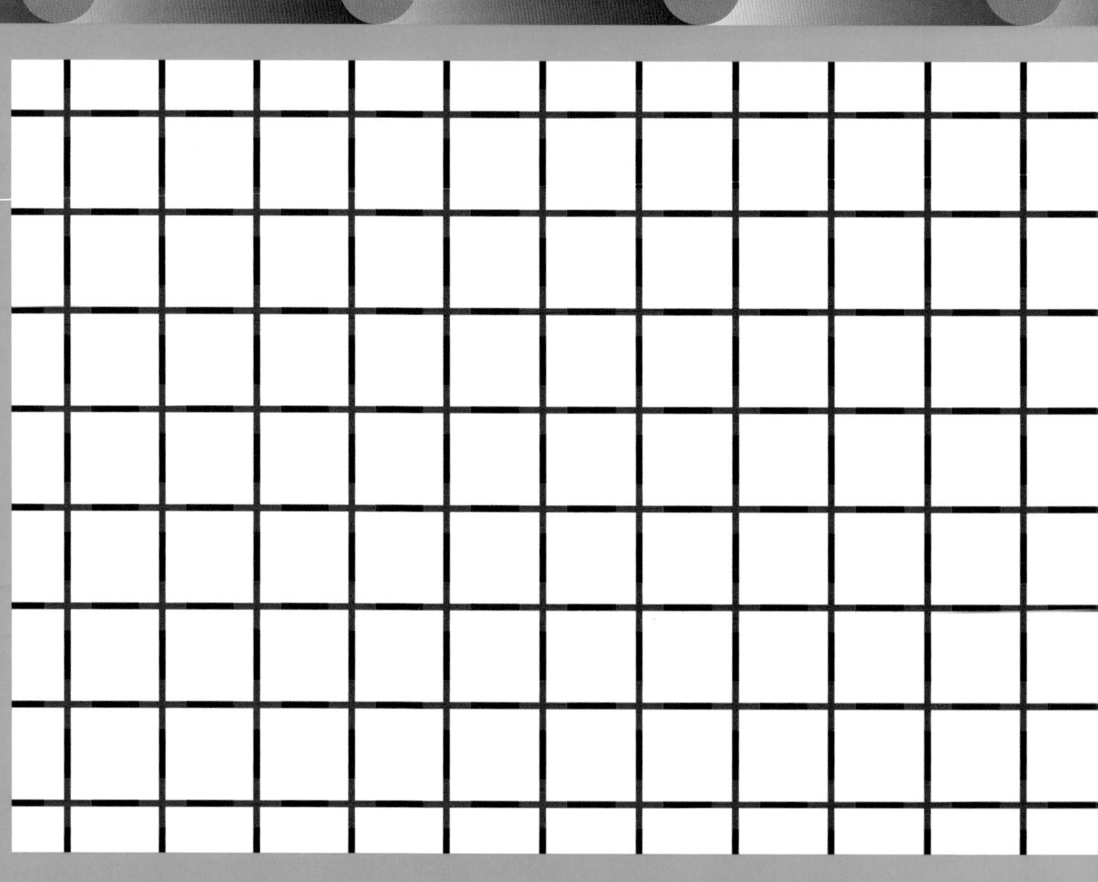

A New Dawn

Do you see shimmering rainbows of color shining out in this illusion?

Move your eyes over the gray tiles on this image and you'll see arcs of color swirling in curved patterns.

So *That's* the Answer

Solutions to queries set and questions posed.

Most of the questions asked in this book are designed to be answered by using the visual interpreter tucked inside the front cover, but there are a few questions that need more specific answers.

Page 15

The vertical center of the triangle is the bottom of the three dots, while the third dot down is the vertical center of the heart. These are also shown in the pictures at the top right of this page.

Page 25

The hidden images are concealed on the pillars. The left pillar contains an image of a black cat, while the right pillar features the top of the Statue of Liberty. Hold the book completely flat and look down the length of each column. They should be perfectly clear.

Page 51

The star is hidden as shown in the image just above to the right.

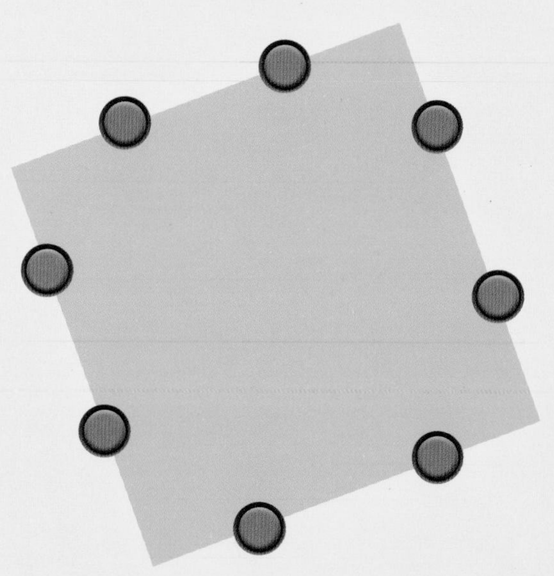

Page 55

The square fits perfectly through the dots as shown in the illustration to the right.

Page 82

There are a total of 11 letter "f"s. If you missed some, go back and work out where they were!

Page 83

The solution to the sum is 4100. Many people incorrectly give the result as 5000 instead.